THE WITCH HUNTER

BLOOD MAGIC
BOOK THREE

JT LAWRENCE

FIRE FINCH

FIRE FINCH

 Created with Vellum

About the Author
JT LAWRENCE

JT Lawrence is a USA Today bestselling author
of 30+ books, and a Kindle Unlimited All-Star. Mother to a
menagerie of chaos, voracious reader, gin fan, and urban
farmer.

*Stay up all night
with USA Today bestselling author
JT Lawrence.*

www.jt-lawrence.com

amazon.com/author/jtlawrence

tiktok.com/@stay_up_allnite

instagram.com/authorjtlawrence

facebook.com/JanitaTLawrence

x.com/stay_up_allnite

bookbub.com/authors/jt-lawrence

pinterest.com/stay_up_all_night

linkedin.com/in/janita-thiele-lawrence-56533610

SPECIAL THANKS

Immense gratitude to my readers
whose loyalty, support, and generous reviews
give me the courage to face the blank page
over and over again.

I wouldn't be able to do this without you.

I hope you enjoy this new magical adventure!

- Janita (JT Lawrence)

THE WITCH HUNTER

BLOOD MAGIC BOOK 3

CHAPTER 1

GRAY SNOW

I need your help, she'd said on the phone. *Could you come in? Today?*

It wasn't the best timing, but is there ever a good time to face an old enemy?

I eased my bruised body out of bed, slowly, as to not wake Darick. I needn't have crept or whispered; he was so deep within his sleep that I was sure an espresso-fuelled marimba band crowded into my small bedroom wouldn't have roused him. Still, I dressed quietly.

The last time he had been hurt, almost killed by a coven of vampires in the volcano pocket realm, he said he needed time to recover. I pictured him as an Alaskan grizzly bear who needed to hibernate in order to heal, and now he was hibernating again. His lacerations were already knitting themselves together, which was no small relief. It turns out that Mages do seem to be able to heal themselves (which was a good thing, especially seeing as my nursing skills are on par with my dancing skills).

After putting a glass of water on the bedside table next to where he lay and checking his breathing—shallow, but steady—I scribbled a note for him and jumped on my motorbike.

I'VE DONE SOMETHING TERRIBLE, Darick had said the previous night, before passing out.

We'll talk tomorrow, I had replied, even though my heart was beating faster, burning to know what he wanted to say. *You need to rest,* I'd said. He tried to talk again but I stroked his face, closed his eyelids, pressed the pads of my fingers to his lips. *It can wait for tomorrow.* I lay back down beside him and fell asleep inhaling the smell of battle on his skin.

READY TO ROAR out of the parking basement, I kicked the stand on my bike and forced my helmet over my head, which felt swollen. I had a hangover from fighting death the day before. I tried not to think too much about it, but the memories flashed in my mind. The train conductor's limp body, his shirt and bowtie dyed heart-ink red. Slyden Abarim drinking my power as I lay, helpless on the vibrating metal floor. Bron risking his feathers and almost losing his life to save me before the *Olde Worlde Railway* steam train smashed into the rock face and exploded into a hundred different hues of flame and smoke. Standing hand-in-hand with Lysander, struck silent as we watched the vampiric pyrotechnic display, bright cinders dancing in the air like fireflies before us. Ash floating down like gray snow.

I shook myself, trying to push away the pictures in my head. I accelerated out of the darkness and into the new morning light, urging myself to feel cheered by the freshness of the day, and the fact that I had survived. On days like this, my bike isn't just a way to get from one place to another; the power of the engine rumbling beneath me and the great blue sky always clears my head. Motorcycle meditation. Plus, Ferra had pimped my smart helmet with such bleeding-edge tech that I sometimes wanted to ride just to play around with the thing. Let me tell you, if you don't have a big-hearted tech-genius surrogate-mother dwarf in your life, you're missing out.

I have been lucky in some ways, I try to remind myself when the grief starts to bubble up like boiling tar inside me. I try to focus on the luck, and not the searing sorrow that is always just one thought, one memory, one hint of a scent, away.

I swallowed hard, and cleared my throat. "Shades," I said, my voice gruff. The safety glass of the helmet's visor tinted a smoked amber. "Weather," I said. "And local news headlines."

"Weather in Johannesburg today," my helmet chimed. "Clear skies with comfortable temperatures and a high of twenty-two degrees. In local news, another Hammerskin attack has left a group of Khargol loyalists in critical condition. This is the third Hammerskin attack reported in the last week. Also, the *Olde Worlde Railway* recovery team has attributed the fatal crash yesterday to a faulty smokebox."

"Ha," I said.

"The Elven Estate has reported an eleven percent increase in overall earnings, which they attribute to excellent fiscal policy and the rise in exports, nationally. And Goblin City management has reported a worker missing. More details to follow."

"No details," I said. I didn't want to hear it. The headlines were depressing enough without digging deeper. So they had found the train wreck, and some bodies. But they'd never know how many vampires were inside when the carriages hurtled into the stone mountain. They wouldn't be able to tell the difference, at a glance, between burnt seat leather and ashed vampires. I wouldn't forget it, though, the fireworks we saw. The multi-colored flames shooting into the sky. Fireworks and fireflies. Gray snow. I shook myself again, trying to dislodge the icy sensation that was inching up my spine.

"Music." I said. "Hellcats."

I accelerated as the dirty rock music streamed out of the helmet's speakers, and I felt it reverberate through my body, along with the thrumming of the loyal engine. I was going back to the Copperfield Institute, and I needed to prepare myself for what I would hear when I got there.

CHAPTER 2
BLUSHED TO BURNING

The outside façade of the Copperfield Institute is generously sized, but plain. It's an understated entrance for what is regarded as the most accomplished magical school on the continent. A large, handsome electric gate truncates the high walls, which are painted a dazzling white that glitters in the sunlight. A bronze-pelted werewolf named Rusty has been the security guard for decades, and he greeted me with his characteristic lupine scowl.

"Jacquelyn Denna Knight," he growled, and then leapt at me, almost knocking me off my bike. He enveloped me in a hug that smelled, even in his human form, distinctly canine, like dog pellets and damp fur.

"I didn't think you'd recognize me," I said.

"I recognize all Copperfield alumni."

Rusty was panting slightly, blowing white puffs of breath in the early morning air, and the glare of the white wall made his eyes sparkle a deep Atlantic blue. His dark lips turned up at the corners as he opened the gate for me. "Plus," he panted, "the Directress told me you were coming."

He bowed and waved me through, and only when I looked down did I realize he had planted a tracking pixel on my trench coat. It was disguised as a visitor badge, but I could practically feel the thing ticking against my chest. Security at the Copperfield Institute had always been tight, but a pixel seemed paranoid. Or maybe there was something I didn't know.

I PARKED my bike under the shade of a giant Jacaranda tree which was bright green with new spring leaves. I remembered it from before, remembered the pale purple blossoms it would rain on us during exam times, promising a positive result. I found myself wondering if today's kids still believed in silly superstitions like that. Like the Kissing Arch twin trees in the third quad, where nailing your shoes to the bark ensured you and your beau would be lifelong lovers. Or putting a white crayon on your windowsill and a silver coin under your pillow to bring on a snow day. We did it knowing full well that snowfall in Johannesburg is as rare as good dental hygiene in an orc's mouth.

There was also the Myth of Minerva's owl. We never could agree on what finding that ephemeral hooting owl hidden in the folds of the robes of the copper statue would get you, but we knew it would be good luck in some form or another. I found the owl one sweltering summer when no one else was around to corroborate my discovery. I was in the tenth grade, and in the difficult transition period between street urchin and Copperfield scholar. I laid my palm on the owl's cool, shaded head, and imagined it cooing softly in the night. The next day, I won the national magical school archery championship. The cheesy trophy still collects dust on a shelf at home: an apple shot through with an arrow. Perhaps superstitions exist for a reason. Untouched psychologists call the phenomena "magical thinking"; perhaps they don't know how close they are to seeing what lies beyond the shimmering veil of the Masquerade.

I made a note to ask the Belore twins if they had found the copper owl yet. I was due to visit them after my meeting, and drop off a bag of Ferra's home baked buttery spice cookies.

A STUDENT RAN down the steps toward me, breaking me out of my nostalgic reverie. She didn't speak, but instead gestured for me to follow her. Sometimes the students agree to periods of silence to concentrate their magic, and I guessed that was what she was doing. As we walked up the stairs and into the building, I made a note to myself to teach Bron that—a simple hack that I had all but forgotten. Staying silent for a few hours or days allows you a deep introspection which can laser-focus your magic. As a cynical, jaded introvert who is terrible at small talk, you can imagine how that appeals to me. But, alas, my line of work involves speaking, as would be evidenced here, in the cool, refined offices of the Copperfield Institute.

The student knocked gently on the blond timber door that stood slightly ajar, and the directress looked up, over the top of her stylish bifocals, and smiled. Sunshine streamed in through the large windows and, just outside, soft leaves all shades of green fluttered like wings in the breeze. The dappled light played on the walls and the polished pinewood floors.

"Ms. Knight," she said, her enunciation as elegant as I remembered from my school days.

I estimated her age to be around ninety-plus, but her face told me a different story. Her dark skin glowed with vitality —*black don't crack*—and her eyes were diamond chips. Her silver-white braids were clipped back with neat metallic clasps.

I had always thought of Directress Copperfield as a titanium woman. Her titanium wand—which lay on her desk before her—was legendary, and she had a spine to match it. Now that her hair was the same color, it looked and felt right.

"Good morning, Directress," I said.

I felt a keen sense of loss, looking at her wand. Mine had been a similar style: vintage, and finely engraved. I had taken it from my mother's limp hand as she lay dead in her bed, and now a vampire had taken it from me. Heartache welled up within me. I knew that coming back to Copperfield would be emotional. It would always be a reminder of what I had lost.

"Please," she said, gesturing at a chair.

I sat down, and the student was dismissed.

"I really appreciate you coming to see me."

She made it sound like I had a choice. Which I guess I did, but I don't know anyone in the Realm who would turn down a request for a favor from Copperfield. I wasn't sure how to reply. *It's a pleasure?* (It wasn't). *You're welcome?* (You're not). *Any time?* (Nope).

This is why I'm bad at small talk. I'm too honest, and not in a good way. I wanted to get this meeting over with and then go visit Eafaris and Pepin.

I sat up straight, and looked into her glinting eyes. "What can I do for you?"

THE DIRECTRESS STOOD up from her tidy ebony desk and walked over to the window, looking out at the rustling trees.

"There's been a death threat," she said, as the leaves whispered their secrets outside.

"What?" I said. "Against you?"

"No," she said, turning to face me. "A Copperfield Institute alumna. She was in your class."

Oh. Of course. The old enemy I needed to face. The directress had mentioned her name on the phone earlier.

"Isadora Crowe."

Izzy Crowe. Spiteful, smug, sexy Izzy. That old witch. After graduation I had hoped to never see her again. Turns out that wasn't going to happen.

Copperfield didn't break her eye contact, making me feel intensely uncomfortable. "Her life is in danger."

A part of me thought, *So what?* My life had been in danger plenty, especially in the last week, and I didn't see the institute recruiting former pupils to help *me*. Couldn't Crowe just fight her own battles? And who wanted her dead, anyway? Did she deserve it? And why was Directress Copperfield asking me, instead of Izzy asking me herself? I knew the reason, of course. Because I would have said no to Isadora Crowe.

"Of course, you'll have your reservations," said Copperfield. "Isadora told me that you two weren't the best of friends."

That was putting it mildly. Once, while I was sleeping, she cut off all my hair during the night. She made it grow back the next day with one of her potions, but not before I woke up horrified, and my skin had blushed to burning.

"But I must remind you that those of us who fight evil must join our light together or be lost to the darkness."

I stared as her words hung in the air between us. "We're not talking about Crowe anymore, are we?"

"There are dark times ahead," said Copperfield, and a shadow scudded over her face like a dark storm cloud.

I felt suddenly chilled. "You feel it, too," I said, and Directress Copperfield turned again to study the garden outside. I followed her gaze and thought about the plant on my kitchen windowsill. It had now grown so much that it was blocking out the light completely, and was beginning to penetrate the cupboards around it and crack the cheap wall tiles along the warped sink. I knew what this meant. The Silvano Clan of vampires were growing in power. They had an unknown quantity of Magus banked, and they had the HighFire Crown.

The future of the Realm was looking dark, indeed. As Ferra would say: *When in doubt, have the cookie. You never know when it will be your last.* And something was telling me that our cookies were numbered. Which really was a shame, because the buttery spice cookies that the Fernak skunks made were probably the best in the Realm. And if there weren't going to be any *Copper Cog* cookies in the Afterlife, then, well, best we try to keep our feet planted firmly in the here and now. My stomach growled then, reminding me of Rusty the werewolf guarding the entrance of the school, and the pixel planted on my chest.

"A death threat," I said. "Can't Crowe come and stay here for a few days, until it blows over?"

Or, even better, move to another country? I thought.

"The security here seems pretty solid." I glanced down at my *visitor's badge.*

"She has important work to do," said the directress. "She can't just disappear from her life. She's the High Priestess of the StarDust Coven."

Important work? That sounds like the name of a pagan domestic cleaning company, I thought.

The White Carpet Vacuumers.

The Moonwash Sisters.

The Witches of the Silver Polish.

"Besides," she said, walking back to her desk. "In my experience, death threats like this don't *blow over*. It's real. I can sense it. And I don't know any wizard who will be a better fit for this job."

I dragged my eyes back to hers.

"I'm not asking you because you were in the same class," she said. "I'm asking you because you have proven again and again what an excellent wizard you are."

"I'm not," I said. "I'm a very ordinary wizard. Mediocre. If anything, I'm a sub-standard wizard."

I'm like that small, bruised fruit on the bottom counter at Spar that doesn't qualify for exportation. That doesn't even qualify for the middle rack. That doesn't even qualify for a JUICY sticker.

"You've always been humble," said the directress.

Honest, more like.

"If you have one failing—" said Copperfield.

One? I thought. *I have hundreds.*

"—it's that you don't know the extent of the power you have."

She meant the darkness. The pain. The lucky curse of grief that augments my power. But why should I use my hard-won emotionally-ignited magic to save the life of a witch who made my life hell in the hostel?

"Because we have to stick together," Copperfield said, as if she had been listening to my thoughts. "Because Crowe is one of us. And because you are the only one who can save her life."

CHAPTER 3
A GHOST IN A GIMP SUIT

"Greetings," said Morgan drily as she fetched me from the reception of the Scorpion HQ. "How the hell are you?"

"Do you want the truth?" I asked.

Captain Morgan pouted her London Bus Red lips and tapped her high heels while she studied my face a little closer than I was comfortable with.

"Maybe not," she said. "Today is grim enough already."

"Do I look that bad?" I asked, knowing the answer.

Morgan froze.

I paused, then, too. "What?" I asked.

"Since when do you worry about what you look like?"

I laughed, a little too loudly. "I'm worried about a lot of things. My appearance generally isn't one of them."

"Liar," she said, but didn't push it. "I was going to buy you lunch. But if you'd prefer to go out for a facial we can definitely do that."

I punched her on the shoulder.

"Lunch it is, then," she said, and hooked my arm with hers. "I've got something to show you."

THE SCORPION HEADQUARTERS' simple buffet-style canteen reminded me of my morning at the Copperfield Institute, but I didn't say anything to Morgan about my new assignment. She had enough on her government-issued plate without thinking about death threats against witches heading up star-what-what covens. Instead I took a deep breath and dug into my lunch, which was a kind of spaghetti bolognese, if spaghetti bolognese consisted of a snarl of old shoelaces doused in a flavorless red sauce sprinkled with a hint of parmesan dust. Even the black pepper I added tasted of nothing, as if it was there for aesthetic purposes only.

"Ah," Morgan said, past a bite of pasta. "They've improved the recipe."

I think she was joking, but I wasn't sure. I finished the food anyway, because when you've lived on the city streets as a kid you never waste food, even when you're in your twenties and the pasta tastes bland.

"So, you're getting laid?" she asked, and I almost spat my last forkful of shoelaces out.

"No!" I said, shaking my head. What I really meant, was, *I wish.* Darick was just layer upon layer of allure. His voice, his rock-solid arms, his bravery. I had gone from finding him infuriating to falling for him, hard.

"Liar," she said again. "You're definitely getting some."

"I'm not," I said, an annoying pink blooming on my cheeks.

"Don't forget," Morgan said, wiggling her eyebrows at me. "I used to be the best detective on the force."

"You're still the best detective on the force," I said, and she shrugged.

"Doesn't feel like it. Not with this V-Cult serial killer case hanging over me."

Guilt hardened the thickness in my throat, making it difficult to swallow. I pushed my plate away and sipped the tepid tap water from my polystyrene cup.

"I've been hearing things," said Morgan. "The Council is getting antsy. They're saying if we don't solve this case soon they're going to reshuffle the squad."

"Reshuffle the squad? They're going to fire you?"

"Probably," said Morgan. "Or disband the Scorpions completely, if they feel like grandstanding."

She acted nonchalant about it, but Morgan's job was everything to her. Losing it would be a disaster. Dissolving the squad entirely would be a terrible mistake, especially with all the trouble on the horizon: the V-Cult killers, the Silvanos, the Hammerskin thugs.

"I'm sorry," I said. "I'm sure we'll get the bastards. I promise I'm on it."

I pictured Liz Durison, then, like I had so many times before. Except that since her apparition visited me in Slyden's enchanted basement I always saw her in her S&M getup. I see latex and whips and steel-spiked stilettos. I'm haunted by a bitter ghost in a gimp suit.

Morgan wiped her mouth and put her knife and fork together. "We've got twenty-four hours before *Flint* can start operating again. Chuck Winnow is consulting, showing them where their potential penetration points are. He told me he'll do his best to help them make it unhackable."

"That's something," I said, remembering the look on Winnow's face when he realized he had been unwittingly aiding a serial killer cult.

"Either way," she said. "The V-Cult is resourceful. They'll find a way to target their demographic."

By *demographic,* Morgan meant *me.* All the victims so far bore a striking resemblance to me, and the candid picture Chuck Winnow had of my face in his drawer was proof that it was no coincidence.

"I'm still trying to work it out," she said, doing that unnerving thing where she stared at me without blinking. "That photograph of you. Why *you?*"

My skin felt cold, then, and I pulled my coat a little tighter.

"Is it a warning?" she asked. "Or a promise?"

I understood, then, that while Morgan was worried about losing her job, she was more worried about losing me. Because all current evidence on the table pointed to the idea that I was on the very top of the V-Cult's hit list.

"I have something to show you," said Morgan. "The reason I asked you to come in."

We left the canteen and made our way up to her office. She rotated her computer screen in my direction and clicked *play.*

"The security team of the store sent this to the police, and they forwarded it to us."

The video was grayscale and grainy. A young man walking, probably in an alley, moving in a strange way. Not striding with purpose, nor ambling. It was like he was listening to music in his head and swaying to it. Then he stopped and fell to his knees, and ripped his shirt open, shouting at the sky. There was no anger in his face, and we obviously couldn't hear the words, but it seemed more like some kind of invocation or prayer. Then there was a black swooping shadow across the lens and it seemed that the man disappeared into thin air.

I frowned. Morgan replayed it. The man was there, and then he wasn't.

"He portaled somewhere?" I said. "Who is he?"

"No portal. No magic. He's not touched."

I watched the clip again. That swooping shadow.

"Vamp attack?"

"There would be a body. Or at least a police report. Instead, when my officers followed up on this they found the man at home, with his family, as if nothing had happened. In fact, reports on vampire attacks are way down."

I found this surprising. "Really?" I had expected the opposite.

Morgan nodded. "Lowest it's been in years. Hardly any coming in at all. And that includes evidence of bleed farms."

I scratched my head. I knew for a fact that the vampires were growing in number and strength. So what was going on?

"And the security footage. The disappearing man. You're sure it's the same guy?"

"Yep. My officers said he was even wearing the same clothes at home as he was in the clip."

"And he seemed one hundred percent okay?"

"Apparently." She looked down at the open file on her desk. "A bit nervous, they said. But they attributed that to being visited by a blue light halfway through his dinner time."

"Weird," I said.

"It gets weirder." Morgan closed the file and reached for a pile of twenty or so more, dropping them in front of me. "This guy is the only one we have on camera, but these other people," she tapped on the top of the pile with her manicured finger, "at one point in the last week or so were all reported missing for a few hours, only to return with no memory of where they were or what had happened in the time they were gone."

I opened the first file and scanned over it. I imagined the people each doing their own thing: sitting at their open-plan office desks, making lunch, chatting with a friend. One second they're slathering mustard on a gypsy ham and cheddar sandwich, then the next second they're gone.

"Like the Rapture," I said. "But they came back."

"A temporary drug-induced Rapture," Morgan said, her lips turning up into a grim smile. "Sounds pretty tempting, actually."

I stopped paging through the top file and looked up at Morgan. "What?"

"I was kidding."

"No, I mean about the drugs. You said *drug-induced*?"

"Not all of them agreed to having their blood tested. Some of them were cagey. We couldn't force them, they haven't broken the law... but when our medical examiner checked Dempsey out—that's the guy in the security footage—the examiner did the standard bloodwork and there was some kind of anomaly. Some red flag. So he tested more and found traces of an unknown psychoactive pharmaceutical."

"An unknown psychoactive pharmaceutical? What does that mean?"

"Look, the examiner is on the force. The regular force. He doesn't know what we do here."

"So you're saying that you think the drug is magical."

Morgan tapped on her keyboard and brought up a visual of what looked like a puddle of rain on oil-slicked tarmac. It was undulating, silver-gray, with notches of rainbow colors at the edges.

"This is what LSD looks like under the microscope," she said, and I nodded. She clicked across and a new picture came up. This time it looked like the cross-section of a globe of ice.

"This is an amphetamine."

GHB looked like a precious stone, MDMA was a dead protea trapped in a soap bubble.

"Now, this is what the examiner found."

Morgan clicked to the next slide and the picture took my breath away. It was a silver snowflake, edged in gold, and fractured inside. It radiated colors that looked bright and deep at the same time, glowing and 3D. Burnt orange and startling blue and saffron. I fought the urge to touch it.

"Wow," I said. "Beautiful."

"All six of the formerly missing people who allowed us to run their bloods had traces of this in their system."

"Do they have previous histories? Of drug use?"

"Some of them do, yes. They're young, healthy. They go to night clubs. They party. They're not *Mary Sues*."

"So it's something you can buy. Something they probably bought or were given by friends. They're not being drugged against their will."

Morgan shrugged. "Difficult to say, but it's a good assumption.'"

"And they're all untouched."

"As far as we can tell, yes."

I stood up and stretched my stiff limbs. "So what do we have?"

"We have untouched people disappearing and reappearing, with no memory of the episode, after taking the new drug on the market."

"A new drug which may or may not be magical."

Morgan glanced at the crazy beautiful snowflake on her screen.

"I think it's safe to say that whatever this is, it's from your side of the Realm."

CHAPTER 4
HAMMERSKINS

I decided to take a walk in the city. Usually, when I feel like a stroll, I choose a leafy suburb, like Blimaex Abarim's neighborhood—Westcliff—with its huge properties and old trees, which were especially beautiful that time of year. But on that day, in that mood, I chose grime over blossoms.

I felt the need to walk the Jozi streets, wanting to see what I could pick up from snippets of overheard conversations and body language. Since my failed mission at The Jupiter Drawing Room I had been feeling off, as if I were somehow separated from my normal reality, stuck in some kind of surreal daydream of vampires and volcanos. I mean, my day-to-day reality had always been surreal, ever since my Mom and Dad showed me how magic worked, but this last week had been especially bizarre. I quickly pinched myself to make sure that I was, in fact, awake. It hurt. I kept on walking.

I strolled past the discount stores with their windows crowded with Chinese wares, trafficking cheap plastic and sweat-factory garments on scuffed mannequins five sizes too small. I moved past beggars and hawkers and smartly dressed businessmen on their way to work, and I could smell the hot oil of the take-away vendors, reminding me of Mister Hot Dog and my old Feral friends. The pavements were strewn with litter, the trash cans boiling over with rubbish. A homeless man lay sleeping under a shop sign that said BARGAIN.

I crossed the chaotic road and headed west. That's when I saw the group of Hammerskins, the morning sun reflecting off the back of their greasy skinheads.

They hadn't seen me. They were busy with something. My immediate reaction was to turn around and disappear in the opposite direction, but then I heard someone yelling for help. The wail was coming from the center of the group of Neo-Nazi orcs.

My body contracted with anxiety. It would be crazy to get involved with a gang of Hammerskins on an ordinary day, never mind a day in which I was wand-less, crossbow-less, and supposed to be solving a serial murder case, a death threat, and a mysterious new Rapture drug craze—not to mention the bloody anarchistic vampires—and it was barely 3pm. I stood there on the pavement, feet fused to the dirty concrete, while the waves of pedestrians streamed past me. I heard another cry for help, and I knew I couldn't ignore it.

I took a deep breath and advanced slowly toward the gang of evil-smelling orcs. Half of them wore stained vests, the other half were bare-chested, showing off their Hammerskin tattoos. I could smell old fishing bait and stagnant water and raw garlic. Barbecue marinade and bile. By the time I reached them my arms and fingers were tingling with fear and potential magic.

The dozen or so orcs didn't even notice me behind them, standing on the tip of my toes to try to catch a glimpse of what was going on inside their bully circle. I'm tall for a human, but standing next to an orc makes me look twelve. It makes me look like one of the mannequins in the shop windows, made in a country where the average person is closer to the size of a dwarf than a wizard.

My fingers itched for my silver wand, my back felt bereft. I tried to keep my breathing even, telling myself I didn't need weapons to win this battle, and only half-believing the words in my head. Finally I caught sight of the victim: a goblin in a sweat-drenched dress. Despite her pleas for the orcs to stop, they kept bouncing her around in their circle, as if she were a slimy soccer ball.

The pedestrians striding past paid no attention. They were untouched, so the fracas wasn't even registering on their radar. My fingers were pulsing now, ready to fight, and my heart was pushing blood through my veins, which felt like they were glowing bright blue.

"Leave her alone!" I yelled, knowing that they'd ignore me. I thumped one of the orcs on the back and he turned around, a stupid leering look on his face. The goblin caught sight of me and started crying, perhaps thinking that she knew she was in trouble before, but now she was done for.

"What want?" said the ruffian, his neck thick and throbbing with sweat and stink. His prison-inked blue-cheese skin repulsed me.

"Leave her alone," I said again, and he laughed, showing me his mossy tombstone teeth. He didn't seem to be armed, but with breath like that, who needs a weapon?

"Maybe she wants to join," said another orc, and the one closest to me grabbed my arm and pulled me into the circle, so that I was side-by-side with the trembling goblin.

"Don't make them angry," she said, eyes swimming. "Please."

The left sleeve of her dress was ripped, and something about that torn fabric made me suddenly furious. I glanced up at the men, ready to sling a spell, when I looked straight into a naked chest that was missing a nipple.

Oh faex.

Perhaps he won't recognize me, I thought, rather optimistically. After all, I had been wearing an orc glamour for most of the time we had been together that sick clammy night in the orc SubRealm. If he hadn't slipped a date rape drug into the *Troll Lager* he had bought me, the glamour potion probably wouldn't have slipped at all. I would have been able to walk out of the beer hall unharmed, and he would probably still have two nipples.

But, alas, the brute's eyes lit up the moment he saw my face. Zargulg remembered me at the same time as I stared at his lone nipple.

"Wizard!" he shouted, and my blood ran cold.

The Hammerskins had all moved closer, and the circle was too tightly knit now to escape. The goblin was shaking so hard I could see her vibrating in my peripheral vision as I blinked at Zargulg.

"Zargulg," I said. "We need to talk."

Talking is not a great orc pastime, but I was grappling for ideas, trying to buy time while I thought of what to do. He sneered at me, then backhanded me so hard that my jaw cracked and my eardrum burst. I grabbed my cheek and took a moment to recover, while the orc next to Zargulg pointed and laughed at my glowing ear, which had started to bleed.

The flash of pain was a shock to my body, and I started shaking, too. But somewhere deep in my mind I was grateful for the gift of the agony, because it shot through my body like an electric current. I was primed to sling a spell before I had entered the circle, but now I was zinging with power, and I knew instinctively that—even without my wand—I could take on every single one of them. I didn't need to gather my force or focus my emotion. My magic was right there under my skin, waiting to be let loose.

"Fiat Fulgar!" I yelled, and a huge bolt of lightning shot from my palm and speared Zargulg exactly where he deserved it. He screamed and grabbed his crotch, and there was the smell of burnt orc skin on the breeze. Then I sent the same spell zinging at his mate, the one who had laughed when he had seen me bleeding. I got him on the ear. The goblin shrieked and dashed behind me while I picked off four more Hammerskins with my lightning spells. My hand was burnt, then, my palm brittle and black, and I knew I couldn't use lightning anymore. The six remaining orcs advanced in a rage, furious that a *girl wizard* had gotten the best of their gang members. The one that had originally pulled me into the circle reached out and grabbed me by the front of my trench coat and picked me up off the ground, and as my boots left the pavement, I kicked the air helplessly.

"Let me go, let me go!" I yelled, and he sneered at me as he had done before.

The goblin in the ripped dress stepped forward and kicked him on the shin, but he didn't even feel it.

"Egh?" he said. He was about to swoop to pick her up, too, but I wasn't going to let that happen.

I looked up at the sky, clustered with solarscrapers and a buzzing helicopter.

"Aversum!" I shouted. Distraction spells are always a bit tricky to get right, mostly because they're highly unpredictable. Unless you're a highly accomplished wizard, you never really know what you're going to get with an *Aversum* spell. Sometimes that makes them fun, but when you have a foul-breathed orc dangling you a meter from the hard-baked concrete pavement it's a bit less so. Nothing seemed to be happening, so I cast it again.

"Aversum!" I shouted, wondering if the deafness brought on by my damaged ear was affecting my pronunciation. Or maybe orcs were just too dumb to be distracted. Or maybe they were so dumb that distraction was their default state of being.

"Urgh?" said the Hammerskin, pretty much proving my theory.

The orc frowned, and I matched his expression. One of the other orcs threw a hessian sack over the goblin and pulled the drawstring tightly shut. The goblin lost it, screeching and flailing about, trying to escape. Another bag was brought out—presumably to grab me—and adrenaline coursed through my body, giving me a fresh round of metaphysical ammo.

"Glaciem Exquiris!" I shouted, and I was so close to my attacker that the spell seeped instantly into his body, liter-

ally icing him where he stood, like a carcass in a deep freeze. Still dangling from his frozen meat hooks—his bratwurst-sized fingers—I leaned over and slung the same glaciating spell at the other orcs, sweeping the freezing energy across them like a giant paintbrush loaded with liquid nitrogen.

You know when you're a kid and you pull ugly faces, and a grownup tells you that you'd better be careful, because if the wind were to change direction while you're pushing the tip of your nose up and squinting like that, you'll stay that way forever? Well, the Hammerskins looked like the wind had changed direction. Their violent body language and cruel, curling lips were frozen as solid as statues. I wriggled and squirmed to loosen the iced orc's grip on my coat, and finally one of his fingers snapped off and I fell down to the ground with it.

Oops, I thought.

I wrenched open the sackcloth bag and let the goblin scramble out. She was holding her neck and hyperventilating.

"Are you okay?" I asked, helping her up, but she couldn't talk past her constricted throat. I changed my angle. "You're going to be okay," I said, and she nodded. She reached up toward my ear and looked sorry that I had been hurt. The anger had left my body, but the pain was still dashing against me in waves.

When I stood up, I almost pitched forward. My balance was off, so I guessed that my eardrum must have burst. When I put my hand to it, my fingers came away slick with blood. I was more hurt than I had guessed. The adrenaline had glossed over the injuries to get me through the battle, but now it was wearing off and my skull felt like it was glowing neon with pain.

I shook my head to clear the stars that were popping up in my vision, hoping my thoughts would clear, too. I started walking away from the debilitated orcs, and the traumatized goblin, who shouted after me. My ear was buzzing so loudly, I couldn't hear what she was saying. I needed to get better, ASAP, but I didn't have time to see a doctor. I had three urgent cases to solve, and I needed an unclouded brain to do it.

CHAPTER 5

POCKET PEBBLE

When I opened the front door of my apartment I hoped to see Darick in the kitchen with a healed body and a sleep-crumpled face, but the room was bare and lifeless, apart from the manic pot plant, which had now cracked its pot in its unfettered desire to take over the world.

I washed the dried blood off my face and neck, then padded through to my bedroom to check on the mage. He was still sleeping, still breathing, rocking a napping Gizmo on his chest. The bruises that had previously looked like floating purple continents on his skin were fading into the background. I had an urge to kiss his cheek, to wake him up, as if I were the prince in the fairytale of Snow White. We just needed Ferra's family in there, I thought. A tribe of dwarfs and an open coffin made of glass.

· · ·

THE DOORBELL RANG, startling me. My nerves were shot from the clash with the Hammerskins, and my skull was still aching. Despite being deaf in my right ear, the doorbell had sounded loud and clamorous, and sent a spike of pain shooting through my brain.

I moved through a cold patch of air, and I could feel Ghost's concern for me.

"I'm okay, Ghost," I said. I didn't have time to feel sorry for myself, and I didn't want the specter's sympathy. I needed to focus outside my pain.

I need a lot of things right now, I thought, *but a visitor is not one of them.*

I sighed and made my way to the door, and when I opened it, it took a while for my distracted mind to make sense of the person standing there. As if the universe had been eavesdropping on my *Snow White* fantasy, there was a beautiful witch at the door with a plate of shiny black toffee apples.

"Halloween's not till next month," I said.

She quirked her lips into a smile, but it didn't reach her eyes. "Hello, Jacquelyn," she said.

I sighed inwardly and opened the door a little wider. "Hello, Izzy."

She held a cat in her left arm, as comfy as could be. Bright peridot eyes shone from its coal-colored coat, which was perfectly camouflaged against Isadora's fashionably tailored witch cloak.

"Poisoned apples?" I asked, looking at the plate in her other hand. The apples were bright green around their stalks, where they had been speared with smooth branches, and the rest of the fruit was perfectly glazed with black.

"Salted caramel," she said, handing them to me. "Delicious."

If you don't say so, yourself.

I waited a moment before inviting her in, making it clear that she wasn't welcome in my house. Then I stepped aside and she swept past me, smelling of burnt sugar and French perfume.

She had the grace to look uncomfortable, standing in the center of my ramshackle lounge, as I put the apples on the kitchen counter. I didn't offer her tea. I had agreed to help her stay alive, not to be her new best friend. Isadora Crowe reeked of money and style, even if it was an eccentric style. I had always felt scruffy around her at school, and the passing years seemed to amplify the effect. She had grown more sophisticated, and I was still wearing the same jeans I had when we graduated. I doubted she wanted to sit in my flea-bitten charity-shop wingback, and I didn't want to acciden-tally injure her by having her sit on a rickety chair, so we stood, instead. She cleared her throat, readying herself to make small talk, which would have been awkward, so I cut to the chase.

"I don't have much time," I said, looking at the time on my phone. "Tell me what you know."

Her cloak and spellstick changed color, then, from black to a peacock blue and green, and the cat's fur changed along with it. It was an amazing effect, like having a large furry chameleon in my sitting room. The cat shook its head and jumped down onto the carpet, loping over to Gizmo's revamped Barbie Dreamhouse where it had a sniff around.

"I've had a death threat," said Crowe.

"Directress Copperfield told me."

"I haven't been able to sleep."

Now that she mentioned it, her eyes did look pretty baggy.

"Tell me about your enemies," I said.

Her eyebrows shot up. "I don't have any."

"I find that hard to believe."

She pursed her lips and stared at me. To avoid her eyes drilling into mine, I walked to the kitchen sink and grabbed a cracked saucer. I poured some water into it and put it on the floor for the peacock-shimmering cat, who hurried over to lap it up.

"What kind of threat?" I asked, and she looked confused. "How was it delivered? Twitter? Phone call? Knock-and-drop? Carrier pigeon?"

At the mention of the bird, the cat looked up and licked its chops.

"A pebble," Isadora said. "In my pocket."

Now it was my turn to be confused. "What now?"

She reached into the pocket of her immaculately cut dress and pulled out an unpolished gray stone with a hole in it.

"A hag stone," I said. "But—"

"We call them adder stones, now," Crowe said. "It's more PC."

"All right," I said, using all the willpower I had not to roll my eyes. "An adder stone. But that's not a death threat. That's the opposite. Hag sto—adder stones—have protective qualities. Especially for witches."

The stones have a naturally occurring hole through them, and according to ancient lore, are believed to have magical powers. They purportedly protect the owner from disease and evil charms, prevent nightmares, and give the holder the ability to see through glamours. Crowe turned the stone over, and the other side was engraved with the elemental symbol for fire.

"Oh," I said.

Maybe it *was* a death threat, after all. The symbol seemed to subvert the nature of the stone, making it the opposite of a protection talisman.

"Someone put it in my pocket," she said in a low voice, eyes wide. "That means he or she was close enough to kill me."

"But he didn't," I said. "Kill you, I mean."

"Maybe he wants to watch me squirm."

"I don't know," I said. "It's hardly a smoking gun. It may be nothing."

"I know that," she said. "I'm not paranoid. But there's something about this," she looked down at the pebble. "Something menacing about its energy. I can't explain it."

She didn't need to explain. I didn't want to admit it, but I felt it, too.

"It's someone you know," I said.

"Maybe."

"Maybe?"

"It was a busy day. I saw lots of people. Went shopping. A stranger could have easily slipped it into my pocket while I wasn't paying attention."

"But a stranger wouldn't have been this calculated," I said. "This is someone who knows you're a witch. They engraved an adder stone, for *faex* sake."

No wonder the woman couldn't sleep.

Isadora Crowe chewed her lip, slightly smudging her perfectly applied lipstick. "So, you'll help me?"

The bright peacock-colored cat meowed loudly, and we both looked at her.

"Yes," I said. "I'll help you."

CHAPTER 6

THE ELECTRON SPIN RESONANCE SPECTROMETER

The dwarf porter at *Mason & Sons* sized me up with narrowed eyes and a distinguished frown as I approached the entrance of the magical apothecary. He was in a maroon suit edged with silver piping, and the tassel on his boxy hat shone even in the overcast afternoon light. The warm color of his suit stood out against the cool black enamel painted walls and window frames of the store. I nodded at him and was about to jog up the two steps to the entrance when a metal gate appeared out of nowhere, blocking my way.

"Wand?" said the dwarf.

"Lost," I said. *Taken by a blond vampire with cheekbones so sharp you could carve carpaccio with them.*

The dwarf remained unconvinced. I couldn't blame the guy, he was just doing his job. Still, it was annoying.

"I was here a couple of days ago," I said.

His expression didn't change.

Oh, for faex sake. I don't have time for this. What would I have to do to prove that I wasn't a muggle?

My irritation made my chest feel itchy, and I directed the uncomfortable sensation toward my fingers. I looked at the gate.

"Volas!" I said, and the obstacle flew up into the air, and I walked into the store.

A SMALL BELL tinkled as I stepped over the threshold. A strange but pleasant mixture of smells greeted me: rosewood incense, pine resin, witches wax, and the smell of burning candles. As ever, the huge store was packed to the ceiling with all kinds of ingredients, potions, salves, and botanicals. And, as ever, the apothecary was watched over by the varnished marble eyes of the giant stuffed crocodile hanging above the counter, who grinned as he observed the goings-on below.

"Lovely to see you again," came a rasping voice from high up, and for a second I thought it was the crocodile who was addressing me. Then I saw the real owner, the fantastically grizzled wizard who had helped me before. He was standing on an excessively tall ladder that leaned against a wall of shelving, which was sighing under the weight of dozens of bottles of golden liquid, tubs plastered with honeycomb logos, and jars of propolis.

"Hello again," I said.

"Bee products," he said, motioning at the jars he was restocking. "They're in fashion. Again."

I wondered how many times bee products would sweep in and out of fashion in his lifetime. My guess was: a lot. He lobbed a small container in my direction; it was the size of a silver coin. Beeswax healing salve.

"Free sample," he said, and hacked a cough into the elbow of his robe.

"Thank you," I said, pocketing it.

I moved to help the ancient man down from the unsteady ladder, but he shooed me away.

"It's not the ladder that's creaking," he assured me. "It's my old bones."

As if that would make me feel better about him plummeting to the stone floor.

As he made his way down the perilous steps, I looked around the apothecary. There was a pile of first aid kits that caught my eye. They were stacked in a haphazard display near the wooden sculpture of a Russian bear intent on hugging a phalanx of mis-matched umbrellas. I chose one of the white metal cases marked with a red cross, and I topped it off with a bottle of ibruprofen. Perfect. I also wanted to pick up something for Darick, but what kind of medicine do you buy a self-healing mage?

"You were so helpful the last time I was here," I said, after the wizard was planted safely on *terra firma*.

"All worked out okay, did it?" he twinkled. "Things have a way of doing that, don't they?"

"I wanted to say thank you."

"Just doing our jobs," he beamed. "I'll tell Grandad you came by."

"He's not around, today?"

"He's taken the day off. Took his new boat for a spin on the Vaal dam."

I guffawed, and waited for the wizard to join in, but apparently he hadn't been joking.

"Did you want another consultation?" croaked the old man, squinting at the antique watch on his paper-thin-skinned wrist. "He should be back soon."

I didn't have time to kick around. "Maybe you can help me?" I said.

"I'll try my very best."

We took our places in the newspaper-walled corner, and I

sat in the antique barber's chair next to the stuffed dodo lamp.

"There's a new drug on the market," I said.

He pushed his glasses up the bridge of his nose and blinked at me. "Oh?"

"A magical substance that has somehow made it past the Masquerade. Untouched humans are taking it, and we don't yet know the consequences. I want to find out what it is, and where it's coming from."

"Well," said the coffin-dodger. "Do you have any for me to look at?"

I shook my head, and the wizard stroked his snowy beard.

"Any idea what's in it?"

"No," I said.

He blinked his watery eyes at me, about to tell me he couldn't help.

"The people that take it seem to disappear for a few hours," I said. "Then they come back with no memory of where they've been."

"Disappear?" he said. "As in, get on a bus?"

"Disappear as in, POOF."

"Hmm," he drummed his bony fingers on his knees. "Could be some kind of portal potion," he said. "Or an *Invisibilis*

Factus philter. But neither of those would wipe their memories."

"True."

"And we should keep in mind that magical drugs don't *accidentally* make their way past the Masquerade." I nodded, and waited as the wizard coughed up some tumbleweed. "I think we can safely assume that some magical person is, for whatever reason, purposefully introducing the drug to the untouched people."

"If I get a sample to you, will you be able to analyze it?" I asked.

"Oh, yes," he said. "Dad's a whiz on the electronic microscope. He's got one of those newfangled ones, with the fiberoptic illumination. And Grandad's just got a spinning machine."

"A spinning machine?" I said. I pictured the ancient man wearing a lycra unitard and neon sweatbands, and cycling in a stuffy gym class to the blare of 80s rock. But then I realized the wizard meant lab equipment.

"When he's feeling fancy he calls it his Electron Spin Resonance Spectrometer, but really it's just a spinner. A standard lab analysis machine."

"Okay, then," I said. "I guess that's what I'll need to do."

Back at the counter, I took my cash out of my pocket and counted some notes out onto the counter. I didn't have much cash left over from the Abarim assignment, but it was money well spent.

At least I had a way forward. I would get a sample of the drug, and bring it here.

"I don't need to tell you to be careful," the old wizard said, looking a little alarmed. "If this person has truly evil intentions, well," he motioned at the first aid case in my hand. "You might need a little more help than that."

CHAPTER 7
VENOM

I waved at the porter on my way out from *Mason & Sons,* and as I gave the dwarf a backward glance, the gold lettering of the store name glinted against the dark paint on the building, as if it was winking at me. I shook some pills into my mouth and swallowed them dry. I climbed onto my bike, unlocking the security enchantment I had placed on it twenty minutes earlier, and ignited the engine with a click of my fingers. Strictly speaking, the clicking bit was not necessary, but it felt good to do it, like when I was a toddler and used my power to clap my bedroom lights on and off. I didn't know it was magic at the time, I just thought that's how lights worked.

My motorbike hummed as I set off down the narrow city street. My ear was still aching, and my jaw made an odd clicking sound when I opened my mouth, but by the time I got home the anti-inflammatories had kicked in and the pain had receded. I parked in my apartment's basement, in my usual spot, next to the Swift entrance and the recycling bins. Instead of taking the enchanted elevator up, I walked around the block to the corner of the building, where I knew I'd find my neighborhood drug dealer.

When Lou saw me, she straightened her hood and almost smiled. "Wizard," she said.

"What?" I asked. "Surprised to see me alive?"

"Yes. There was a rumor about a gang of Hammerskins who were beaten up earlier. By a *'girl wizard.'* I assumed it was you."

"Deodamnatus," I said. "They'll be after me, now."

As if I didn't have enough enemies in the Realm.

I looked at her ebony face and matching dreadlocks. Her quinine iris seemed brighter than ever, flickering from within the dark shade of her hood.

"I have a question," I said.

"Of course you do."

"What's that supposed to mean?"

She shrugged. But I knew what she meant. I only ever approached her when I needed help. I had been in survival mode this past week, doing only what needed to be done to stay alive, and I hadn't worried about bruising anyone's feelings on the way. I thought perhaps that was why SaltySnap was cold toward me the last time I saw her, when we went on the Safari Ride together. She hadn't called or texted me since then. I made a mental note to bring her a gift: rainbow popcorn with extra salt. Or maybe I would take her for maple syrup pancakes and a lime milkshake at that awful coffee shop at Goblin City.

"I still owe you for the medicine you gave me," I said. I used the term "medicine" lightly. They were more like hallucinogenic troll-strength painkillers. "They worked really well. Thank you."

Lou shrugged it off and looked away at the street which was now crowded with hooting traffic and hawkers. Exhaust fumes and vernacular colored the air.

"I mean, they really helped, and I'd like to pay you back," I said. "Is there anything in particular you need?"

"Not yet," she said.

"Let me know, when you do."

I wondered if I would come to regret saying that. But, fair is fair.

"To answer your question," Lou said, dusting a piece of flint from her jacket. "Yes. He was here."

"I haven't asked my question, yet." Then I registered what she'd said. "Wait. Who was here?"

"That vampire. The hot one that was here before. Blondie."

Lysander. My stomach leapt, and not in a good way.

"When?"

"A couple of hours ago. He was looking for you."

"He asked for me?"

"No."

My heart beat a bit faster. "He was just skulking around?"

"Kind of. So, I asked him what he wanted. He said he had something for you."

Had something for me? What? A bullet? A pair of fangs? Would it be insanely optimistic of me to think he would return my wand? Or—

"I offered to keep it for you," she said, "but he wanted to deliver it himself."

Hope and dread mixed together, painting my insides a toxic yellow. I never knew where I stood with Lysander. Talk about a dysfunctional relationship. I'm a proficient vampire slayer, and he's a vampire. At the very least, it made things a little awkward.

"But that wasn't your question," Lou said.

"Right." I took a deep breath. I tried to pull myself together. Having an extremely good-looking vampire problem was pretty far down on my list of urgent issues to resolve. Lou kept looking at me, waiting.

"The new drug on the market," I said. "I need to buy some."

Lou shook her head. "Nope."

"It's not what you think."

"It doesn't matter what I think. You're not going to get it."

"Why not? You don't sell it?"

"I don't sell anything I haven't tried myself."

"Don't tell me," I said, blood draining from my face, and the toxic yellow glowing brighter like a bulb about to burst. "I need to go back to EverShade."

"No," said Lou, shaking her head. "You must never go back there."

I never wanted to return to that evil black magic market for as long as I lived.

"Besides, you won't find any Venom there."

"Venom?" I said. "That's what it's called."

"Yes," she said. "And it's not for wizards."

"Who is it for?" I asked. But I already knew the answer.

"Listen hard, Wizard," she said, every trace of friendliness gone from her face. "You do not want to get involved in this. Do you hear me?"

I heard her.

"Don't start to think you're invincible."

"I don't," I said, touching my cheek. I wasn't close to invincible, and I had the cracked jaw to prove it.

CHAPTER 8

THE SCREAMCOASTER

"**G**ood. You're here," I said to Bron, who was waiting patiently outside my front door, practicing his Latin incantations.

My orc security guard, Gnor, was asleep, as usual, and he didn't stir as I opened the door and we went inside. Gizmo ran to greet us, and Bron picked him up and stroked him.

"Hello, Gizmo," Bron giggled, and it reminded me how young, and tender, he was.

"Hello, Ghost," I whispered, as I moved through a cold patch of air on my way to the bedroom.

Darick was still unconscious, but he was looking much better. He had more color to his face, and his skin was completely healed and smooth. Nothing like mine, which sometimes reminded me of a crazy quilt with all its bruises and lacerations, and old scars, each one with its own memory. I was damaged goods, and I knew it. If only Darick could heal psychological trauma, too.

I packed the new first aid case away and changed my shirt, which smelled like city smog and stress-sweat, then went back to the lounge to find Bron playing with Gizmo in his Dreamhouse and feeding him scraps of biltong. Gizmo was tearing his way through the beef jerky as if he hadn't eaten in days, which may have actually been the case.

"I thought he was a vegetarian," I said, and Bron laughed, even though I hadn't been joking.

I caught sight of the candied apples on the kitchen counter: still perfect, green and black and poisonous-looking.

"You want a toffee apple?" I asked. "A witch on a hit list brought them over."

"No thanks," Bron said. "I was hoping to make it through the day."

"Yes," I said, turning my back on them. "Me, too."

We caught a tuk-tuk to Goblin City, and I phoned Morgan on the way.

"It's called Venom," I shouted into my phone, amongst the hooting and blaring of the five o'clock traffic.

Her voice popped and crackled down the line. "What?"

"That Rapture drug. It's called Venom."

"Got you."

"If I can get a sample, I'll be able to tell you what's in it. Then maybe we can find out who's making it, and why."

The tuk-tuk was rickety and seemed to be held together with box tape, superglue and string. A miniature disco ball hung from the cracked rearview mirror, and the tinny sound system assaulted us with a terrible goblin rendition of *Only the Good Die Young*.

"How are you going to do that?" asked Morgan. "Find a sample?"

"I'm not sure yet. I have a contact, but... she won't stock it."

"A drug dealer with a conscience?" Morgan mused.

"Something like that."

There was a pause in conversation as our tuk-tuk overtook a communal taxi and almost crashed into an oncoming smart black sedan. Our driver hooted at the car and flipped him the bird, even though he had been the one driving like an orc.

"Take it easy!" I shouted at the driver, who ignored me and put his foot down.

"What?" said Morgan.

"Sorry. Our driver thinks he's bloody Evel Knievel."

Bron cast his jade button eyes at me. Maybe I should have made him fly there, after all.

"Morgan, before you go," I said. "I need a favor, please."

We skipped a red light and almost plowed into a bicycle. Our driver swerved just in time, and scraped the side of his tuk-tuk wheels on the high pavement, swearing and smacking his steering wheel as the cyclist took his time in crossing the road.

Deodamnatus, I thought. *My nerves were scratched enough. No more tuk-tuk rides for me. From now on, Bron can fly, and I'll ride.*

"I have another case," I said to Morgan. "An old school acquaintance of mine is in trouble."

"What do you need?"

"Can you check if there've been any prior incidents..." The line buzzed and broke and then came back again. "Anything to do with witches being targeted."

"What now?"

The red truck in front of us stopped suddenly, and Bron and I held each other back to avoid tumbling forward into the back of the suicidal driver.

"She's a witch," I said. "She received a very witch-specific death threat."

"I have no idea what you're talking about," said Morgan.

"Just look for any kind of report of witches being threatened or killed… for being *witches,* I mean."

When we reached our location, the tuk-tuk screeched to a stop, and I banged my knee, sending a sharp, spiteful pain up my leg. The billboard-sized sign on the outside of the old amusement park said GOBLIN CITY.

Morgan yelled over the static. "Let me get this straight. You're looking for a witch hunter?"

"Yes," I said, grimacing. "Yes, I guess so."

FROM THE OUTSIDE, Goblin City looked bereft: abandoned, defaced, left to decay. That's exactly the way the goblins wanted it. They wanted untouched humans to drive right past and not even register the place, despite its size and terrible past.

But when you stepped inside, everything changed. It was like stepping from a black-and-white world into technicolor, and from a silent film into a jarring blast of rushing sounds: shrieking rides, excited chatting, and peals of goblin laughter. Smells, too, of *boerewors* rolls and vinegar chips, and vanilla ice-cream dipped in molten chocolate that cracked against your teeth when you ate it. It's the smell of the fresh donuts that always gets me, but usually I resist. Bron was with me this time though, his eyes wide and bright, so I caved and bought some for both of us, and we ate them as we waited at the ScreamCoaster for Nilve Salty-Snap to arrive for her shift.

Dozens of goblins stood patiently in the queue for their turn while the others shrieked as they raced and tumbled. When the clock struck six p.m., the goblin on duty cricked her back and stretched, ready to go back to the hotel, or maybe out for dinner at one of the many themed restaurants in the park. But when her replacement showed up, it wasn't Salty.

I stood up and wiped my fingers on my paper serviette. "Hello," I said to the new goblin.

She looked at Bron and I suspiciously. "What do you want, Wizard?"

"I'm looking for Salty," I said. "This is her shift. Nilve SaltySnap."

SaltySnap was by far the most proficient portaler I knew, whereas I sucked at it. Bron needed to learn Portal Magic from the master. I was going to ask her to teach Bron the basics while the ScreamCoaster whizzed around on its tracks, then they could do a practical lesson after her shift.

I had tried to arrange the lesson beforehand, but she hadn't been taking my calls, and my text messages remained unseen and unanswered. When I couldn't get hold of her, I thought that perhaps if I just showed up and appealed to her, and paid her upfront, she'd have a hard time refusing.

But this wasn't Salty standing in front of me, in her Goblin City uniform and newly sewn on ScreamCoaster badge.

"You haven't heard?" said the new goblin, and her sneer softened.

"Heard what?"

"It's been all over the Realm news."

My stomach flipped. "I don't listen to much news," I said. I have enough trauma in my own life without throwing in with the rest of the world.

"Nilve was a great goblin," sniffed the one who was just knocking off work.

"What do you mean, *was*?" I asked, my voice high.

The rollercoaster barreled past us with a trail of delighted screams, then rocketed up into the circular track above us.

"SaltySnap is missing," the replacement goblin said. "She just disappeared."

CHAPTER 9

A RAGE OF ORCS

"We have a problem," I said to the orc who was twice my size and made my athletic legs look like cheap matchsticks. The orc looked down at me. He could snap me in half without even trying. Perhaps I needed to be a little politer. "... Boss," I added.

He was standing in the late Godfather's office at the back of *Cucina Or'Capone,* the Khargol family restaurant, in front of the wide gas fire that gave the cave-like room a cozy feel, despite the obvious menace in the air. He was warming the back of his legs and playing with an ornament from the mantlepiece, a large smooth black oval rock that looked like it might be a fossilized dragon's egg.

"Hello, Wizard," he said, and I felt appropriately embarrassed by my lack of manners, especially seeing as the man was paying for security at my place 24/7. The least I could have done is greet him before launching into a rant.

"Gnor is making problems?" asked Boss.

I didn't know the head of the Khargol security team's real name, I don't think anyone did. Everyone just called him "Boss" and he seemed happy enough with that.

"Gnor is fine," I said. Sure, the guy sleeps a lot. And he let a strange vampire into my apartment when I wasn't there. Plus, he dislocated my shoulder by accident the other day... but he's not a bad orc. He keeps my stinky landlord away, which is a perk that cannot be underestimated. And I had the feeling that if something really dangerous happened, he'd be up and at 'em. It was a good feeling knowing I had an orc in my corner, even if he was narcoleptic.

"I'm talking about the Hammerskins," I said.

"Ugh," said Boss, his face twisted up in anger and disgust. His arm started shaking and I saw that he was unknowingly squeezing the dragon egg in his palm. I hoped he wouldn't crack it. Instead, he turned around and slammed it back onto the mantle, cracking the gray marble.

"They're getting out of hand," I said.

"Out of hand," he murmured. I could feel the fury coming off him in waves.

"They're going around in groups, terrorizing people. That attack on the Khargol loyalists yesterday. Seven orcs were killed. And this morning they were trying to kidnap a goblin off the street."

I thought of her ripped dress, and I didn't even want to guess what they were planning on doing to her. And I didn't want to guess what they would do to me, either, once they tracked me down. Because I knew they would. Not only had I hurt them, but I had humiliated them in broad daylight. Everyone in the Realm knows that orcs take both pride and vengeance pretty seriously, and I assumed it was doubly true for Neo-Nazi orcs. I knew without a doubt that it was just a matter of time before I had a rage of orcs storming my door. Especially the crotch-scorched Zargulg, and the particularly vicious orc whose frozen finger I had accidentally snapped off. Our looming reunion would not be a pretty one.

Boss was still turned away from me, perhaps watching the flames. A honeyed portrait of the late Don Vito hung above him. Oversized, overly-flattering, and framed in gold. This kind of errant behavior would've never happened if he was still alive. We both knew that, and it made Boss as mad as hell. Or'Capone would have shut the Neo-Nazis down immediately and without mercy. He wouldn't have stood for any kind of uprisings or rebellions in his tribe; he was known for taking out entire families of dissidents, children included. It seemed cold-blooded at the time, but now I saw the bigger picture. If we allowed the Hammerskins to overthrow the existing Khargol rule, it would wreck the Realm. I had the feeling that Boss was a more moderate guy, which was good in general, but not good when dealing with psychopathic skinheads intent on destroying the Realm's rocky status quo.

"A friend of mine is missing," I said. "A goblin." I suddenly felt emotional and had to swallow the thickness in my throat. "I'm worried she's been taken."

Boss turned around.

"I'll see what I can do about that," he said. "If the Hammerskins have her, I'll make sure she's returned safely."

So he was moderate *and* optimistic. I didn't fancy his chances of survival much, never mind holding onto his precarious position of power. A blush crept up my neck and bloomed on my cheeks. Maybe it was the heat in the room, or maybe it was the dawning knowledge that the Realm was going to be totally, utterly screwed. The Hammerskins were rising up like nefarious weeds, and soon they'd be choking out the rest of us. I pictured blood on the streets and smoke in the air. Our eyes connected and we held each other's gaze. A civil war was coming, and there was nothing either of us could do to stop it.

CHAPTER 10
THE STARDUST COVEN

When Isadora Crowe had asked me to attend her coven's moonlit gathering, I immediately thought of around a hundred things I'd rather do, including sharing breathing space with an orc, being French-kissed by a goblin, and going for a bikini-wax/root-canal combo special at my local Thai spa. But Izzy did have a point. It was the perfect way to meet the people in her life and get to know a little more about her and the StarDust Coven. It would be awkward and uncomfortable, but it may lead to finding the first domino in my witch hunter case.

You'd think that witch hunting was out of fashion now, seeing as it had already been done to death—RIP pun-loving Qwynkle—up until the end of the Salem trials, but there are still psychopaths out there, looking for an excuse to kill innocent people because they don't agree with their worldview. Witch hunters, in my opinion, are one of the worst kinds of psychos, because they pretend to be all holier-than-thou, condemning women who have seized power for themselves, when really they're just looking for an excuse to murder. And the last time I looked, murder trumped a little spell-slinging in the evil stakes every day of the week and twice on Sundays. I'm no shrink, but I'd bet the most valuable possession I own—which, granted, would probably struggle to fetch a hundred bucks at the neon-pink pawn shop on Eloff Street—that the witch hunting malarkey is just a veneer for some extremely deep-seated psychological issues. They may think of themselves as agents for the good, ridding the Realm of evil witches, but I believe that far more evil lurks inside a witch hunter than it does a witch.

I didn't want to attend a moonlit coven gathering, and I certainly didn't want to do it at midnight, at a disused chapel in a spooky, cordoned-off park dense with pine trees and rocks in the shapes of the creatures who creep and scuttle in children's nightmares. Why did witches have to be so damn eerie? Why couldn't they just be like normal people and meet over coffee in a nicely-lit restaurant where there was wine and food and somewhere to pee?

Nope. Instead they chose a post-apocalyptic-looking chapel in the middle of a park I'd never even heard of—

That's the point, said Crowe. *So that no one will disturb us.*

Waiters at nice restaurants don't disturb you, I wanted to say. *They just bring you whisky and nice things to eat.* I could even arrange to book the private dining room at *The Copper Cog & Ale,* I said, and have steaming plates magically appear, but she didn't buy it. I didn't know what she had planned. Perhaps they needed to slaughter a goat or something, and I guess that wouldn't go down well at any establishment, not even at Ferra's steampunk pub for magical creatures.

So, against my better judgement, I made my way to the secret park—Isadora had sent me a location pin which confused my *Forage* Maps and scrambled my GPRS, but then it led me there, anyway—which was great because I hadn't brought Gizmo along. I was being more careful with Gizmo, now that I had him back; there was no way I wanted to lose him again. Apart from being my beloved pet, I thought of him as my secret weapon, and decided that from then on I'd only use him when I absolutely had to. In the meantime, I let him swan around in his refurbed Barbie Dreamhouse and eat popcorn, as magical albino ferrets are wont to do.

I parked my bike, which was warm from the ride over from *Cucina Or'Capone,* and thought how very dark the forest surrounding me was. The pine needles were fragrant as I bruised them underfoot. I made my way toward the chapel, which was glowing with lunar light; it shone like a beacon from within the black branches and brush. The building, though broken-down and abandoned, seemed to assert a certain magnetic pull, a halo of enchantment, and then I begrudgingly admitted to myself that perhaps this *was* a better location than a pulled-pork hipster joint in Parkhurst.

That didn't mean I didn't think it was creepy. It was still as sinister as hell, walking up that weed-fenced track, stumbling on stones, hearing things scurry across my path. I almost walked into a spidery thing hanging from a branch, which immediately gave me PTSD-like flashbacks from my seemingly never-ending night spent in *Obsidian Hill Cemetery*, but then I saw it was a kind of dreamcatcher, a pentacle fashioned from pine shoots. My scream stuck in my throat.

Nothing to see here, I told myself, pushing it aside and walking on. *This isn't creepy at all*, I thought. *Nope, no sir.* Then I heard a cackle in the distance, and my hair stood on end. *Blair Witch Project, anyone?*

CHAPTER II

OLD ENEMIES

When I reached Moonlit Chapel I could hear people talking in hushed voices inside, and the interior was dimly lit with the licking flames. There must have been a hundred candles there, stuck with their own melted wax all over the broken building's interior. The place was scented with gray smoke: burning wicks and hot wax, a smell I've loved as long as I could remember.

The witches were all wearing black cloaks and standing in the entrance hall. I almost blended in with my trusty dark genius-dwarf-designed trench coat. Which reminded me: I needed to see Ferra as soon as possible to get a new magical heat-seeking crossbow, and see what she could do about a new wand for me. She knew what the antique silver heirloom had meant to me, knew what I needed it for, and she was the most talented engineer I knew. Still, I knew deep down that nothing would replace my mother's wand. I still had my father's pentacle ring, which was too big for any of my fingers, so I wore it on a silver chain around my neck. At least I still had that. It was something.

"Jacquelyn," purred Isadora. The old witch—I mean, *High Priestess*—came forward and clasped my hands in hers, as if we were dear friends, instead of old enemies. By the way she was gazing at me, you'd never suspect that she'd put self-tan in my hand lotion right before the Copperfield Institute prize-giving ceremony, or wood glue in my hair conditioner before the Summer Solstice dance. "Thank you for coming."

A witch's cloak is not designed to be sexy, but on Izzy it looked boss, and her make-up was perfect. Only Isadora Crowe could look sophisticated in a sack cloth. All right, it wasn't a sack cloth. It was a beautifully tailored cloak the color of ink, and it was shot through with gold glitter, as if someone had sprinkled the dress from the top. It was a bit flashy for a witch's robe, but I guessed the glitter was supposed to symbolize the stars. When I looked closer, I saw that the stars were moving, ever so slowly, as if they were based on actual stars in our Milky Way. They fizzed and faded against the night sky of the fabric. It was mesmerizing to watch. When I looked into her eyes I saw them sparkle there, too, and I thought she looked composed and right and utterly beautiful. I realized then that I still hated her a little bit. It was childish, but it was true. One day I'd be a better person, but that day was not today.

"Isadora," I said. Most people would have smiled and played along. I am not most people. I wanted to get on with everything, and that did not include pretending to be friends with someone I really would rather not have seen ever again. It had been a long day, it was almost midnight, and I wanted to get back to Darick, who I was sure was close to waking up. "Can we start?"

Isadora's cat looked me up and down. She was as black as Crowe's cloak, and she had the sprinkling of the roving star glitter, too. Her irises were as bright green as ever.

"Of course," Crowe said, her smile tightening, the fluid movement of her fake friendliness turning brittle before my eyes.

Isadora Crowe clapped her hands gently and the sound reminded me of a raven taking flight: the *snap-snap* of wings working against the wind.

"Let us take our places," she said, and the other witches who had been milling about and chatting in hushed whispers gathered around, smiling and nodding. Apart from Crowe, there were eleven witches there, nine women and two men.

"Paige," said Crowe, smiling, "you may begin."

Paige, a tender-faced woman of around nineteen or so, was Crowe's second. She nodded and took the broom that leaned against the vandalized wall, and used it to sweep the concrete floor at the front of the chapel while the others watched in silence.

"Hazel," said Crowe, "please go ahead."

A cross-looking witch walked over to the just-swept floor and used one of the hundred candles that decorated the ruined building to light the bouquet of dried herbs in her hand. The smudge stick caught alight and sent perfumed white smoke billowing into the cool night air. The sweet-smelling scent of the white sage reminded me of the interior of the magical apothecary, *Mason & Sons.*

With the little church freshly swept and cleansed of bad energy, it was time to move past the old timber chairs stacked at the back, which I couldn't help thinking were a bit of a fire hazard. We all headed toward the front, where the candles painted the chipped plaster with their flickering colors of yellow and orange, and their movement made it look like the pentagrams and elemental signs drawn there were moving along with them. The cross-looking witch, Hazel, put the still-smoking smudge stick into a clay vase and out of our way.

"Fidelis," said Crowe, smiling at one of the older witches, a tall, slender woman whose cloak only reached mid-calf and gave the impression that she had grown overnight. Fidelis smiled back and rummaged in her scruffy bag, bringing out a piece of magical chalk. She strode with purpose out in front of us and cast a perfect circle on the dry, gray concrete screed floor. The coven moved toward the circle without having to be told, and stood along it, toes touching the line.

Isadora Crowe put her cat on the floor and spent a few moments looking at each member, acknowledging them, making them feel welcome and necessary to the night's proceedings. The gold-flecked cat made a beeline for the side door, lined with glowing candles, and disappeared outside. The coven waited in a patient silence for every witch to have their turn in the High Priestess's beam. Normally I would have felt annoyed, but it gave me time to take in each witch's face. Crowe had texted me a list of the coven members after our first meeting. There was Isadora's assistant, Paige Periculum, and the tall, older woman, Fidelis Wolfmoon. The cross-looking one was Hazel Shackleton, and I thought then how her surname suited her locked-in face. The man to her left was Erik Tenebris, who was Hollywood-handsome. You'd think that standing next to a man with a body like that would cheer the old hag up, but it seemed to have the opposite effect. The woman on the other side of Tenebris was Violet Maleficum, and then there was the married couple, Ophelia and Dylan Knox. Their matching cloaks looked new compared to the witches on either side of them, and their star glitter glinted cheerfully, which also seemed to make Shackleton cross. Every time she looked in their direction her eyes narrowed and her lip curled. I wouldn't take it personally, if I were them, I thought. If her eye daggers when she looked at me were anything to go by, that sneer seemed like her default expression.

FINALLY, the High Priestess began to talk. "May life thrive, now and always," she said. "The circle is ever open, never unbroken. May the Goddess awaken in each of our hearts. Merry meet and blessed be."

"Blessed be," chanted the witches in return.

"Hettie Frost is not here," Crowe said. "That is unusual."

The witches nodded in agreement.

Fidelis Wolfmoon looked concerned. "She hasn't missed a StarDust gathering before."

"She didn't say she wasn't coming," said Paige.

"Perhaps she's just running late," murmured Violet, looking at the watch on her wrist.

Fidelis glanced at her own watch, what looked like a cheap flea market trinket, and shook her head. "Hettie is never late."

I saw uncertainty, perhaps fear, flicker on Isadora's face. I could tell she was thinking of the pebble in her pocket. "Paige," she said, a little breathless. "Phone Hettie. See if she's okay."

Paige brought out her phone and scrolled for Hettie's contact number, the white lighting up her face, and the technology looking out of place in the warmly lit chapel. I noticed that her fingers were trembling ever so slightly. Crowe must have told her about the death threat.

"A mobile phone!" scolded Shackleton. "At a coven meeting! Whatever next?"

A couple of the witches rolled their eyes. Paige found the number and clicked to dial. They all waited while the phone rang and rang.

A couple of the witches began talking at once, including Fidelis and Tenebris, who both asked at the same time: "Should we be concerned?" and Shackleton said, "Is there something you're not telling us?"

"No answer," said Paige, although she didn't need to.

Isadora took a deep breath and put one hand on her chest while she exhaled, and she held the other hand out to quieten the coven.

"I'm sure Hettie is okay," she said, not sounding sure at all. "But we do have something troubling to discuss."

The Knox couple looked at each other with concerned expressions, and Tenebris frowned, his eyebrows joining together in worry. Violet glared at me as if I were responsible for Hettie Frost's tardiness, and I glared back. Bloody witches. I'd had enough of them already. The panic and the politics. *Thou shalt not suffer a witch to live,* said that guy in the Bible (I forget which), and I kind of understood where he was coming from—about the suffering part, anyway. We hadn't been there for long but I was already tired of standing in a drafty chapel, waiting for a latecomer to arrive, while they freaked out around me. Even at school the witch contingent irritated me; they were always so highly strung. I'd pray to not get too many of them in my homeroom class. On the back of the restroom door outside the potions lab someone had scratched and inked into the wood: WITCHES BE CRAZY BITCHES.

Extremely sensitive to energy, Crowe would say, I'm sure. It's all about the atmospheric vibrations with witches, which made times like these especially challenging for me. My jaw began to hurt, and I realized I was clenching it. They were like scrabbling hens, squawking at an imagined axe man in the coop. I may have imagined it, but I thought I saw Dylan Knox look a bit irritated too. We caught each other's eyes and his lips twitched; a hint of a smile, and I returned it. His wife looked on, wide-eyed and oblivious to our exchange.

"What is it?" asked Violet, "what do we need to discuss?"

"I have an old friend here, tonight," said Crowe, and the witches all quietened down and looked at me with such interest that I squirmed.

Old enemy, more like, I thought. *How convenient memory can be, how easily the past can be glossed over, turning foes into friends.* And then I told myself to get over it, because I was on a job there and then, and it's best to not get distracted by long-forgotten vendettas.

"Jacquelyn Denna Knight is the best wizard private-eye in Johannesburg," said Crowe, "and she's agreed to help us."

"Help us?" said Shackleton, the grumpy witch. "Why do we need the help of a wizard?"

I saw in Hazel Shackleton's face then a flash of despair, as if an old reel of disappointment was playing in her head. I wondered if she had wanted the position of head of the StarDust coven, but was beaten to it by Crowe. Perhaps she disliked Izzy as much as I did. That wouldn't do, being a witch. Witches live by the maxim that whatever you do comes back to you, and that philosophy does a good job of keeping them on the straight and narrow. Wishing evil on your coven leader, even subconsciously, would not be a good idea.

Older generations of witches and wiccans say that whatever you do will return three-fold. The younger witches don't put it as delicately, saying *karma is a bitch*, or *it will come back to bite you on the ass.* Either way, most witches believe that doing evil is never worth the potential repercussions.

"There is something I need to tell you," said Crowe. "And I don't want you to be alarmed." She plunged her hand into her pocket, presumably to get the engraved adder stone, and the witches stared and tittered. Paige dialed Hettie Frost's number again. Crowe's cat hissed and yowled from outside, and Izzy's head immediately snapped in the direction of the sound.

"Celestine?" she called. "Celestine?" and when her cat didn't come, Crowe broke the circle and rushed outside.

CHAPTER 12

EARTH

"Celestine?" Isadora called. She was standing outside the ramshackle chapel when I found her, staring into the black edged trees. "Celestine?"

The other witches streamed out into the darkness, and with them, a fine white mist appeared, isolating us from one another. "Celestine?" they started calling, and making the *skss-skss* sound that cats seem to like. I haven't had much experience with pets in my life. A Feral friend, Wandile, used to try to tame the occasional rat, but she never had much success. She said you needed treats to train an animal, and we were short on those. I had always wanted a pet, I'd thought it might help the chronic creeping loneliness, but I didn't like the idea of a creature being dependent on me. It was too much responsibility, and in my line of work I could never guarantee that I'd survive the day. I wasn't sure that my odiferous orc landlord would approve, plus I didn't need another mouth to feed. My cursed fridge is desolate enough as it is. But of course, sometimes you don't have a choice. I didn't choose Gizmo, Gizmo chose me, and now I couldn't imagine life without him.

"Celestine?" I called. I could hardly see the other witches. The ones closest to me were just creeping silhouettes. No way we'd find an errant cat in these kinds of conditions. I looked back at the chapel, which, now blanketed with mist, took on an ominous appearance.

ISADORA HAD BRIEFED me on the significance of the Moonlit Chapel earlier. It used to be a sweet church, *like a gingerbread house,* she said. Which I thought was a funny thing to say, for a witch. People had used it for small weddings and christenings. It was painted white inside and out, and had beautiful stained-glass windows in the pointed arch frames that ran along the sides. Colored glass that would light up and sparkle when the sun shone through them, and paint the floor with rainbows. Ivy used to grow up the sides, sometimes pushing itself through one of the small, open windows, and the clay vase used to be filled with the wildflowers that grew all around the property.

Then, overnight, something happened. When the groundswoman came to do her usual maintenance work one day, she found the wildflowers surrounding the chapel flattened, and the stained glass smashed so thoroughly that not a pane remained in place. There was no sign of vandalism, no graffiti on the walls—yet—and it seemed to her that something more sinister than human-led destruction had occurred. Her suspicions grew when she investigated further and found a wide path of burnt grass leading away from the building. She followed it, and came across a clearing in the trees that had not existed before. A wide circular pattern the size of a rugby field had been burnt into the grass where the trees had been felled. It didn't look as if it were created by humans, she said, and mentioned that she got chills standing there, got so cold in the middle of summer that she didn't think she'd ever get warm again. I felt empathy for the groundswoman then, even though she was probably dead and buried by now. I knew that chilled feeling, that cold despair, and I hoped that she had found her way back to warmth after she had left the strange sight.

THE GROUNDSWOMAN REFUSED to return to work, and as the word spread, people decided they didn't want to say their vows and douse their babies in a haunted church, so they stayed away, too, and the chapel fell into disrepair, only to be used by passing vagrants and... the StarDust Coven. Today the crop circle is still there, albeit covered slightly by the surrounding weeds and flowers, but the grass where the pattern was burnt into the ground has never grown back.

Isadora doesn't think of the crop circles as ominous. They haven't hurt anyone.

Yet, I remember thinking, when Crowe was telling me the story. They haven't hurt anyone *yet.* I thought they were as creepy as hell, especially as we stood around, calling for the missing cat.

"Celestine?" I called, walking over the soft black soil, trying not to trip in the dark. "Here, kitty-kitty."

Damn it, I should have brought Gizmo, I thought. And something about that thought nagged me and nagged me, whirring around in my head the way my thoughts do when they want me to take notice of them. There was something I was missing, and it felt urgent.

Gizmo? I thought. *Spooky crop circles?*

The witches all around me were calling for Crowe's cat.

Celestine had wanted to stop their moonlit meeting and get them outside the chapel.

Why?

Then with a shudder I put it all together, and my blood ran cold. The soft dark soil, the nagging thoughts of Gizmo, the engraved adder stone in Crowe's pocket, the reason the cat wanted us outside.

"Paige!" I shouted. "Paige!" and the young woman came running, her face white under the glow of the waning moon.

"Phone Frost again," I said, "phone Hettie Frost again."

Paige looked confused for a second but did as she was told. Isadora came running, along with some of the other witches. When they reached us they stopped suddenly and looked at us askance.

"Did you find her?" Crowe asked. "Did you find Celestine?" But she could see that we had not. She stared at me with electric eyes: fear and loathing in the haunted chapel yard. Paige found Hettie's number and clicked to dial, and we all waited in silence and dread.

"It's ringing," Paige said, but she needn't have, because under the soft black soil—the freshly-dug soil—we could hear Hettie Frost's phone ringing.

CHAPTER 13

TEARS TURNED INTO INK

"*Faex!*" I shouted, and the witches around me exclaimed in shock, too, although none of them in Latin, which I guess is their loss more than it is mine. I find that swearing in an ancient language is a uniquely satisfying experience. The phone kept ringing underneath our feet, and then I leapt into action.

"Ambulance!" I shouted at poor Paige, who was now as white as the mist that surrounded us and was in danger of disappearing altogether. She started dialing with shivering fingers.

"Find tools!" I shouted at the witches. "Anything we can dig with."

I fell onto my knees and began to shift the soil with my hands, pushing my fingers into the cold black earth and scraping the skin off my hands doing so. I thought of my nightmarish visit to the *Obsidian Hill Cemetery* and realized why Gizmo had kept popping into my head. In that spooky pocket realm, he had shown me the way to the unmarked grave of Ametrix Belore and made me dig him up. And now, even though Gizmo wasn't physically with me, he was showing me the way to Hettie Frost.

The men, Knox and Tenebris, dropped and joined me in the digging, as did Isadora. We were like wild animals, then, digging as if our lives depended on it.

"We're coming, Hettie!" shouted Crowe. "You're going to be okay."

Shackleton and Violet appeared with spades, which I found excessively fortunate... suspiciously so. When I frowned at Shackleton she said, "They were around the back of the building."

I didn't have time to ask questions. The men grabbed the spades.

"Nano spade!" I said, cursing myself for not thinking of it before shredding my hands in the rocky soil and wasting precious seconds. The four of us dug as fast as we could, throwing the dirt out beside us. I found a small black object —Hettie's phone—and tossed it out. Then we hit something hard. The men slowed down when we saw the shape of the thing.

"Hurry!" I shouted, even though I knew why they had

slowed. The chances of anyone surviving being buried alive in a sealed coffin were slim to none.

"Ambulance?" I asked Paige.

"On their way," she said.

I wiped the sweat off my face with my dirty hands and I could feel the mud smear over my skin as I did so. My arms were on fire and my palms were blistered, and I supposed that I was slowing down, too. Isadora grabbed the nano spade from me and took over, grunting as she heaved shovelful after shovelful of soil out of the pit. If it didn't work out as a High Priestess for a magical domestic cleaning company, I thought, she may have a future in professional tennis. The lid was soon free of the heavy earth and Knox was able to crack it by stabbing the spade just under the lid and levering it open.

Scarred by my experience at Obsidian Hill, I shielded my view, expecting rats to jump out and squeak at us, and maggots to squirm and squelch, but Hettie Frost's body was free of vermin.

Hettie's body held its own horror: the tips of her fingers were worn down almost to the bone, the bottom of the lid was scratched and painted with her blood, her face and limbs were blue with oxygen deprivation.

"Hettie!" screamed Isadora, losing all sophistication and restraint as she clamored into the casket with her friend, sitting her up, trying to pull her out. She lost traction and slipped, falling onto the body. I planted my feet firmly in the mound of soil and offered her my hands, and Dylan Knox joined me in pulling both Crowe and Hettie out of the grave while the other witches looked on, horrified.

I kneeled down beside her and checked for a pulse and any hint of a breath. There was none. Hettie's blue skin was cool to the touch, but I began chest compressions anyway. I pulled my hand into a fist and slammed the bottom of it down onto her chest, then I laced my fingers together, heels down, and began pumping the witch's breastbone with all the weight I could offer, counting as I did so. After five compressions, Isadora pinched Hettie's nose shut and gave her mouth-to-mouth. Hettie's chest ballooned and fell, ballooned and fell, and then I started the compressions again. My own heart was beating so wildly in my chest I could hardly hear anything. It was just Hettie's blue body, and Crowe and I working in prefect rhythm, and everything else disappeared, apart from the mist that was still rolling and swirling around us.

Tenebris tried to cut in, to give me a break, but I shook him off. If I just kept going maybe Hettie's heart would kick into action. Her mouth remained slack, her body limp. Looking at her worn down fingers made me cringe. Compressions, counting, breathing. Compressions, counting, breathing. Compressions, counting, breathing. Crowe gave no sign of giving up and I rode the punishing path with her, not giving up until she decided it was time.

Feeling for her pulse again, this time on her wrist, I saw in one of Hettie's hands an adder stone. While Crowe was breathing into her lungs, I picked it from the witch's palm and looked at the engraving. Isadora and I saw at the same time that it was the elemental symbol for *earth*. I heard Paige sobbing, and a few others muttering in anguish and fright.

Shackleton stepped forward. "She's dead," she said, but Isadora kept trying, and so did I. My arms and shoulders were burning, my knees were numb.

THE WITCHES ENGAGED in some hushed talking, then disappeared inside the chapel. They returned with a candle each, clasped in both hands, and formed a circle around us and the gaping hole in the earth. They began to chant, and the combination of their flame-lit faces against the dark night and the mist swirling around us was evocative and moving, and spooky as hell. It was some elaborate incantation, one I didn't know. As they chanted in unison, I felt the humming of their voices deep in my body. I hoped it wasn't any kind of necromancy, because any flavor of magic that attempts to raise the dead is invariably dangerous to everyone involved. Their spell-work became louder and faster, and the humming zipped up my spine, almost taking my breath away. I glanced up at the witches and saw their eyes were all liquid and black, as if their tears had turned to ink, and as their chanting increased in volume, I felt the energy rising in the air, as if it meant to float us all. Crowe and I kept working at the CPR, and when I looked at her face, just a breath away from mine, her eyes had turned black, too, and it struck fear in my heart. The chanting reached fever pitch, until I didn't think I'd be able to stand it any longer, then there was a loud gust of fire as the flames on each candle grew and burst before us, lighting up the ground and Hettie's pummeled body for a moment, and in that overblown moment Hettie gasped and scrabbled at her imaginary coffin lid, then sat bolt upright, wheezing and choking, and looked right at me with her wet black eyes.

CHAPTER 14
WHAT THE FAEX

The wail of the ambulance in the distance snapped everyone out of the weird surreality. It was like tumbling down from some kind of plane, back to the soft black earth that had suffocated Hettie Frost. A gale snuffed out every candle, and washed away the magical residue from the faces and eyes of the StarDust Coven. Regular eyes blinked back at me now, as I stood and Crowe and I hoisted Hettie up and carried her still-stiff body into the chapel, where Fidelis and Violet had made a bed for her.

"Hettie!" shouted Isadora, completely exhausted, "Hettie!"

Hettie didn't move, didn't blink. Her skin was still blue, but she was alive.

Celestine, Izzy's cat, came running in from outside, and Crowe grabbed her and hugged her to her chest, planted her trembling lips to her head, and stroked the dead leaves and soil off her galaxy-colored coat.

"Good girl," she muttered, Hettie's adder stone still in her palm. "Good girl."

The whining of the ambulance siren stopped, and we heard slamming of doors. A few moments later, three paramedics ran into the chapel. If they thought the gathering of witches in a haunted chapel was an unusual sight, they didn't show it. They slammed a black stretcher on the concrete floor and moved Hettie's stiff body onto the sturdy fabric.

"Name?" one of them demanded.

"Hettie Frost," I said.

The chief paramedic clicked his fingers in front of Hettie's face, but she didn't blink. He clicked his penlight and looked into her eyes, but her pupils didn't contract. I watched his face pull in a concerned way.

"Hettie," he said. "Hettie. Can you hear me?"

She didn't react.

"Do you know where you are?" he asked, as the other men tore open the plastic and paper packaging of needles and tubing. The man with the red hair slapped the crook of her arm, looking for a vein. He jammed in the IV needle while the darker-skinned man shoved an oxygen mask over her face and turned it up to its maximum setting. The sound of the air hissing filled the chapel. They wrapped a space blanket around her, the silver fabric rustling as they tucked it into place. I could smell the oxygen that escaped the mask, and I could smell my own trauma and fright, mixed with mud. My fingernails were black.

"Lift!" said the chief, and the other two hoisted up the stretcher at the same time, moving swiftly to the ambulance.

"I'll come with you," said Crowe, visibly shaken. She'd need some treatment, too, I thought, once they had sorted Hettie out. She was clearly in shock, pale as paper under a film of soil that all but covered her, and her teeth were chattering. The paramedic glanced at the cat in her arms and looked as if he were about to say something about no animals being allowed in the ambulance, but then he took in her grim state and decided to look the other way.

"All right," he said, giving a curt nod. "Let's go."

WE HEARD the emergency vehicle's doors slam shut and the engine and siren started up again. We listened to the ambulance speed away, leaving us standing in silence. I think everyone was thinking the same thing, and that was *What The Faex?*

The witches had arrived for a peaceful moonlit meeting and then things went south so quickly we were left breathless in all senses of the word. I found myself staring at the pentagram spray-painted on the graffitied wall.

"You did a good job," said Dylan Knox. "You saved her life."

"I don't know," I said, shaking my head. I didn't know if she would make it. Yes, we had forced her heart to start beating again, but sometimes a beating heart is not enough. And how much of it was resuscitation, and how much of it was the creepy spell-work they had done? I wasn't even close to understanding what kind of magic they had performed, and I wasn't sure I wanted to, either. I thought of the engraved adder stone that had been clasped in Hettie's hand. A death threat, Isadora Crowe had called it. Hettie's stone was carved with the elemental symbol for earth, and Crowe's had been fire. It was clear to me then that the threat was very real. I looked around at the rest of the coven: pallid faces and worried eyes. Paige was crying in the corner, being comforted by Fidelis and Ophelia. Would they all receive a stone? I didn't like this. I didn't like this at all.

I SLEPT TERRIBLY, despite having Darick's body in bed to keep me warm. I had nightmares about being buried alive and suffocating slowly, slowly, slowly, while people walked over my grave. When they finally noticed I was missing, they dug me out, but by then I had been chewed up by starving rats and my skin was a stew of maggots. I woke up choking on my own vomit. As I hugged the toilet bowl at three a.m. I felt overcome with the darkness in the world, the evil and pain and the suffering, and if it weren't for Darick and Gizmo I wasn't sure I would've decided to carry on, so intense was the dark dagger in my heart.

It felt hopeless, and I felt a keen longing for my parents. I would have done anything to see them again, feel their arms around me. I was like a brittle bone, and only the love that I had lost would be able to soften me, but there was no chance of that happening. There was more chance of my crashing to the ground and shattering, and the destructive part of my psyche told me to go ahead and smash myself. It would just be a matter of time, anyway, till someone else did it. And wouldn't I prefer to be the leader in my own demise than have someone else break me? A Hammerskin, perhaps, or a hungry vampire? The V-Cult killers were always hovering at the periphery of my life, and now I had the witch hunter to deal with, too.

When I finally had the energy to stand, I padded through to the kitchen for a glass of water. I saw that the plant had totally broken out of its pot now, which lay in shards and crumbs of soil on the cheap tiled floor, and had covered the entire wall with its voracious tendrils and glossy leaves.

Something inside me snapped, and instead of destroying myself as I had been previously tempted to do, I launched at the plant, pulling it down despite its stubborn grip on the wall. Chips of paint and plaster came down with it, pock-marking the wall. Uragh, my landlord, would not be happy, but I didn't give a flying *faex*. I ripped into it, unwinding the thick creeping vines and attacking the base with a rusty pair of kitchen scissors. I tore into the plant as if it were personally responsible for putting Darick in a coma, as if by killing the plant I could destroy the pocket realm it symbolized, even though I knew it didn't work that way. Because every day the plant crept and grew meant that the Silvano Clan's pocket realm was increasing in power, and that frightened me more than any Hammerskin or witch hunter.

Once I had lacerated my hands and exhausted my limbs, I dropped down to the grimy kitchen floor and leaned against the cupboard under the sink. The tiles were covered with torn branches and stripped leaves, and the darkness came for me once more.

"It's the medieval fair today," said Isadora Crowe's gruff voice. I could hear she was phoning from the hospital; there were sounds of beeping medical equipment and rattling steel trolleys.

My eyes were scratchy from an awful night's sleep, and I had a kind of bone-deep exhaustion that I could only cope with by ignoring it. I had spent the last hour sitting by Darick's bedside, urging him to wake up. I didn't like to admit it, but I needed him. I was feeling starkly vulnerable and I couldn't bear it; it was like walking around without skin.

"The medieval fair?" I said, confused.

"You need to go."

My shoulders slumped. Witches clearly didn't know that *medieval-anythings* were like honeytraps to vampires, and, for once in my life, I wasn't in the mood to deal with vampires. Or, for that matter, witches dressed in kirtles and bonnets and velvet gowns that dragged in the mud, and apple-cheeked men in dirty tunics and shoulder clasps, swilling badly-brewed mead and eating suckling pig off the bone.

"How is Hettie?" I asked.

Crowe hesitated. "The same," she said. "Critical, but stable."

"Conscious?" I needed to ask her some questions.

"Hardly," said Isadora. "I mean, her eyes are open, but—"

"Okay," I said. "Call me when she's talking, will you? She's the only person who can help us."

"She's still blue," said Crowe. "No matter how many blankets I put on her. She's still cold."

"We need her to wake up," I said. "See what you can do."

I realized I was coming across as ruthless, but Hettie Frost was the only one who could tell us who the witch hunter was. To add to the urgency of the situation, I was pretty sure that the witch hunter knew Hettie had survived, and would speed up his plan to kill the rest of the StarDust Coven before she healed enough to be able to tell us what had happened.

"You need to go to the fair," said Crowe again. "The killer will be there."

My breath caught in my throat. "How do you know?"

"I just do," she said.

It made sense. If there was a witch hunter in town, he'd be checking out the local talent at the biggest pagan-gothic festival on the Jo'burg calendar. He'd be there, in costume, and he'd be watching the goings-on very carefully. I'd have to be there, too, to try to get some kind of handle of this situation. At that moment I had nothing except two engraved pebbles and a deeply traumatized coven.

I rubbed my face. The skin on my palms was still blistered from digging and scratched from attacking the plant in my kitchen. What I really felt like doing was lying down next to Darick and forgetting the rest of the Realm existed.

"All right," I said. "I'll go."

"Thank you," she said, her voice cracking. I realized that after we had spent that time resuscitating Hettie and working so well as a team that I no longer disliked her. I had seen how single-mindedly she had dug and how hard she had worked to save that witch's life. I had never respected Isadora Crowe, but I did now.

"Call me as soon as Frost wakes up," I said.

WE HAD all been pretty shell-shocked after the previous night's events, and I hadn't asked the StarDust witches any questions. Today I had to force myself to focus. I decided to interview the witches one at a time to attempt to get an idea of who would want them dead.

I arrived at Fidelis Wolfmoon's house without warning and parked my bike. It was a quaint old house with a pretty garden, sweet peas and ranunculus, pink daisies and navy blue tulips. A climbing rose covered the trellises on either side of the house, and I could smell their scent as I moved through the garden and rang the doorbell. Seeing nature so happy here almost made me feel guilty about hacking my kitchen plant to pieces. Almost.

The witch didn't come to the door, but her car, an old Toyota Tazz, was in the garage. Perhaps she was taking the day off and not answering the bell. The Void knows I wouldn't blame her. I needed a duvet day, myself. I needed a whole twenty-four hours at home reading, sleeping, and bingeing on Netflix and Ferra's cooking. I needed a day off to give my muscles and my mind a rest. But today was not that day.

I rang the bell again and rapped on the door. The wind chime tinkled merrily in the breeze, and I pulled the trench coat tighter around my body against the chill. The sky was bright blue—perfect for an open-air festival—but the winter chill in the wind had not quite left the city yet.

"Fidelis!" I called. "It's Jax. From last night."

Still nothing, and I didn't want to waste the trip, so I stretched out my arm and put my palm on the handle.

"Ignem Exquiris," I said, under my breath. I used just enough of the fire magic to force the lock, and the door swung open with a protracted squeak.

"Wolfmoon?" I called. Perhaps she wasn't wearing her hearing aid.

The house looked in perfect order, and had a warm, lived-in feel. Photos of children and grandchildren were framed on the wall, and the small fireplace had not yet been cleaned of the previous evening's cinders. On the dinner tray next to the couch lay a half-knitted jersey for a baby. It was blue and yellow, and had the picture of a sailboat on it. The only cause for possible concern, I noted, was a mug of cold tea that sat on the kitchen counter, a thin film on its surface. A hint of lipstick, the faintest pink, marked the lip. Now, I let cups of tea get cold all the time, so I was not immediately worried. But then I saw the poison apples.

A platter of Crowe's toffee apples sat speared on their plate, perfectly green, and perfectly glazed, exactly like the ones Isadora had given me when she had visited my apartment. And they, like my apples, remained untouched.

"Fidelis?" I called. Perhaps she had gone for a lie-down; she would have been tired after last night's events. I wended my way past her kitchen and down her passage, in the direction of her bedroom, checking what I guessed was the spare room on the way, crowded with craft supplies and a quilting machine.

I tapped on Wolfmoon's bedroom door, then gingerly it pushed open. "Hello?" I said.

The last thing I wanted was to catch her off guard. Or, worse: off guard and naked. But she wasn't in her room, and her bed was neatly made. I looked around, tentatively, not wanting to invade her privacy—which was an optimistic aim, as I was already standing, uninvited, in her house, in her bedroom—but my need to find out more about the Star-Dust Coven was more pressing than my desire to not disturb her.

The breeze was blowing into the room, and the voile curtains billowed and swayed. There were sounds of Spring outside: birds tweeting, leaves rustling, and a particularly enthusiastic neighbor with a lawn mower. I walked up to the window and shut it, and there was instant peace and quiet. Only then did I hear it. The sound itself was innocent enough, but for some reason it razed the peaceful feeling in the room and curdled my insides. I moved toward the sound of the dripping tap.

CHAPTER 16

ADRIFT

The sound of a dripping tap would not usually make my nerves flare, but I knew immediately that it was more than that, and my breath caught in my throat. I took a quick look around, checking for intruders, but the only one I saw was my reflection in the scalloped vanity mirror. Closer, closer. My heart started beating hard and fast; a 1900s racehorse on cocaine. I stopped and took a few deep breaths to calm it, but it galloped along as if it wanted to break out of my chest entirely.

The dripping was louder now, and I was just a few steps away from the *en suite* bathroom. By then I knew something was definitely wrong, but when I saw Fidelis I was still taken aback, and I heard my own gasp, too loud, as if it had come from someone else beside me.

I rushed over to the bath and plunged my hands into the freezing water, my movement causing the water to spill over the edge and splash onto the tiles below. I slipped and then recovered as I wrenched Wolfmoon's body up, shoving my hands under her arms and lifting her so that her head surfaced, but she did not take a breath. I heaved her body up and out, dragging her onto the floor, soaking myself in the process and not even feeling the wet or the cold.

In the split second I had seen her alone in that porcelain bath she had seemed at peace. She was lying on her back, fully dressed, eyes staring through the clear water at the ceiling, her hands crossed over her chest. I smashed that veneer of deadly calm, shouting at her to wake up, slapping her face, turning her on her side so that the water could run out. But just before I was about to administer CPR I noticed she was still wearing her watch. A flea market bargain, not waterproof, and its face told me it was just past seven a.m. When I looked at my phone for the time, it was nine fifteen. The witch had been dead for over two hours. No amount of chest compressions would bring Fidelis Wolfmoon back to life.

I called Morgan with the address, then covered Wolfmoon with one of her thin, embroidered bath sheets. I sat with her on the wet bathroom floor for a while, cradling her head and holding her hand, thinking of the little baby that would never get his hand-knitted jersey with a sailboat on it, or another hug from his grandmother.

When I heard the rumbling engine of Morgan's SUV pull up outside, I stood up. My legs were stiff. That's when I saw the pebble in the bath. I reached once again into the water, but stopped myself just in time. The forensic team would be here soon, and I had already trampled over all kinds of potential evidence. Best to leave the stone where it lay. I didn't need to hold it to know that it was an adder stone, engraved with the elemental symbol for water.

CAPTAIN MORGAN TOOK one look at me and blanched. "What is it?"

I was dripping on the grass lawn where I stood. "One of the witches," I said. "I think I'm going to need your help."

She threw a towel over my shoulders and sent her forensic team in, and they bustled around in their white uniforms and stockinged feet, taking fingerprints and photographs as they worked. I stood shivering in the cheerful garden, telling Morgan about the previous night's StarDust Coven gathering, about finding Hettie Frost buried alive, about Isadora Crowe's death threat, and the three adder stones. Standing in a pretty garden made the whole experience feel even more surreal, remembering the swirling mist and dark-leafed trees, the heavy black soil that almost killed Frost.

"I'll send a team to guard Hettie Frost's hospital ward," said Morgan, taking her phone out of her pocket.

"Did you find anything?" I asked her. "Any other recent murders of witches?"

"We're still looking," said Morgan. "You know what it's like. We don't have the resources for jobs that aren't briefed in through the system, so it's moonlighting or nothing."

"Yes," I said, looking down at the grass beneath us. "I know what it's like."

"But now that this has been reported," she made eyes at the house, "it'll be investigated. Officially, I mean."

"By you?" I asked, and Morgan looked uncomfortable and looked away.

"Maybe," she said. "There's a new detective on the block. Maybe he'll get assigned. I don't know yet. But I promise you that I'll follow up. I'll go in right now and see what I can find."

"A new detective?"

"Council-approved," she said. "Or, more like, Council-mandated. He just kind of swooped in and hit the ground running, telling everyone how to do their jobs. You know, the jobs they've had for years while he's been in the unit for less than twenty-four hours. The Powers That Be have already given him half of my cases."

"They're grooming him to be Captain of the Scorpions?" I asked.

Morgan sighed and curled her fingers into a fist. "Looks like it."

"Deodamnatus," I swore.

I didn't know what was up with the Council lately. I know we're not supposed to ever doubt the Council, or criticize them—they have all that power for a reason—but they don't seem to have been functioning optimally. When I had hot-lined that I had Slyden Abarim locked up in his basement, they never contacted me, and as far as I know, they never arrived at his house to arrest him. Also, they had been extremely quiet on the Hammerskin uprising, and I had expected them to have taken some course of action by now. Yes, they were pretty much all-knowing, all-seeing, with their agents on every corner of the Realm. Maybe there was a bigger picture, a plan I wasn't seeing, but their inaction left me puzzled. Also, everyone knew that Morgan was by far the best detective the Scorpions had ever seen: honest, hard-working, bright as a pin. If I was allowed to criticize the Council, I would say that they were in danger of making a big mistake.

"What's his name?" I asked.

"Tilexon," Morgan said. "Tilexon Musubarin. Quite a mouthful."

"Wait," I said. "He's a wizard?"

What was the Council up to?

"The team doesn't know," she said, "it would make them jumpy. It's one thing investigating magical crime, but I don't think they'd like the idea of having a wizard for a boss."

"I HAVE SOMETHING FOR YOU," said Morgan. We walked over to her SUV and she opened the passenger door. There was a large gift on the seat wrapped in blue wrapping paper and bound with a gold-colored ribbon. The illustration on the paper—copper cogs and pistons—whirred and ticked away.

"It's not my birthday," I said. Although, to be honest, I didn't know when my real birthday was. I had a date given to me by the Copperfield Institute, but the real day remained undocumented, and when I thought of that it made me feel a little unmoored, and adrift. I was already feeling shaken up by finding Wolfmoon's dead body in the bath, and thinking of my early childhood intensified the emotion.

"It's from Ferra," Morgan said, but I knew that already, having recognized the gift wrapping.

"When did you see Ferra?" And, more importantly, I wanted to ask, *Why?*

"Just this morning. She said I should be sure to give it to you as soon as possible."

My hands were still trembling, and I knew I'd battle to untie the ribbon. I clicked my fingers at the parcel. *"Monstras,"* I said, and the ribbon untied itself, and the pretty paper peeled away to reveal a new crossbow.

"Oh, bless that dwarf," I said. I wouldn't be alive without her. I picked up the shiny new crossbow—the third one Ferra had printed for me this month— and looked through the scope, which was clear and wide and beautiful. I pulled on my back-strap and clicked my new weapon in place. Having my crossbow made me feel immediately better. Stronger, and less vulnerable. I may have lost my mother's silver wand, but I had a magical crossbow designed by a tech genius of the dwarf variety. When I counted my blessings, Ferra was always on top of my list.

"Don't forget the cookies," said Morgan.

I didn't understand what she meant, but then she motioned to the seat, where a bag of Ferra's spice cookies lay among the shredded blue paper.

CHAPTER 17
KRESNIK

I stood at the entrance to the medieval fair and girded my loins. I never liked attending these kinds of things, with the dress-up and the play-acting. I know a lot of people think it's fun, but I've never been a big fan of games, especially when vampires are involved. And at events like this, vampires are always involved.

I had enough on my plate without having to kill some rogue vamps; I was pretty sure the witch hunter would be at the fair. I had to find him and stop him before he killed any more StarDust Coven members. I also had to get hold of some Venom, although I didn't know how. I needed to get it to *Mason & Sons* for them to tell me what it was, and then maybe we'd be able to find out who was distributing it, and why. Then, of course, there was Liz Durison, the dominatrix in my dreams, tearing her shirt open to show me her V-Cult branding, and whipping the table with a loud *snap*, telling me to get on with finding her killers or die trying (I hoped it wouldn't come to that, but the odds didn't seem to be in my favor). Durison was getting tired of living out in Limbo Land. And, as her stilettoed gimp-suited ghost liked to remind me, it may be too late for her, but I still had a chance of survival if I found the killer cult in time. I knew I was *numero uno* on their kill list. I just didn't know when they were planning on striking.

I've got ninety-nine problems, I thought to myself, *and being on top of the hit list of a vampire killer cult is just one of them.*

"Welcome! Welcome!" yelled a man, and blew through his dented brass trumpet, making me jump. "Welcome to the Medieval Fair!"

He was dressed in a grubby linen shirt that he was wearing under multiple tunics, and his legs were sheathed in bottle-green leggings. He wore a wide leather belt with a flashy copper buckle around his potbelly, which looked like it had seen its fair share of roast turkey and mead. On his head was a silly hat with a black feather in it, which gave me an idea.

I pulled out my phone and speed-dialed Bron, hoping that he was up for a lesson.

Within five minutes a raven darted overhead, and I watched as it flew against the brilliant blue of the crisp African sky, then circled down toward me. It flew into a nearby tree, perched on a branch, and angled its head at me, staring with its alert, beady eyes. Then it dropped lower in the tree, so that it was obscured, and soon I saw a small brown hand curl around the bark of the tree trunk, and then Bron's naughty street urchin face appeared, green eyes reflecting the morning light. He was clearly happy to have been summoned, and I was grateful for the help. He gave the word "wingman" new meaning.

"Ready for a lesson, Bron?" I asked, and he nodded. I thought then that when I bought myself a new wand—I had been putting it off, forever hopeful that I'd get my mother's back—that I'd buy one for Bron, too. He had put in so much time and hard work into learning magic, it was time for a reward. Not to mention the fact that if he could focus his power, it would help me, too, especially in sticky situations. In the meantime, I'd give him something else.

He stepped in the direction of the medieval fair's entrance, and I shot out a hand to stop him. I pulled him back.

"Bron," I said, and he looked up at me with his sparkling jade buttons. "You're a good student. You're doing really well. I'm proud of you."

"Thank you," he said. "Thank you, Jax."

"Not to mention the small detail that you saved my life on that train."

"I was just returning the favor," he said, and smiled with all his teeth. "You saved me from the dragon."

A needle of guilt pierced my side. I wouldn't have had to save him from that fire-breathing chimera if I hadn't created it in the first place.

Ah, well, it was inconsequential, now. No-one's perfect, right?

"I want to give you something."

"It's not necessary," said Bron. "You're teaching me. That's all I want, you know that."

Oh yes, I knew that. The boy had pestered me for weeks before I finally resigned myself to the fact that he wasn't going anywhere, and that I may as well take him on as the apprentice I never knew I needed.

"I'm going to give you a name," I said.

His eyes grew wide. "Really?"

"Really," I said. "What's your surname?"

"I don't have one." Of course he didn't have one; he had never been given a chess-piece name that would brand him for life as a Copperfield orphan. Well, I would name him after his special ability.

"Kresnik will be your new last name," I said.

"Kresnik?" he said, tasting the word in his mouth.

I thought it tasted of straight vodka and borscht. Maybe Solyanka soup. It certainly had an eastern European flavor.

"I realize it sounds slightly—"

"I love it!" he said, hugging me, and I was reminded by his small, slender frame of how very young he was, and the needle was back in my side. But there was no going back, now. I needed Bron Kresnik as much as he needed me.

I paid for the tickets and a roving map. Then we walked, arm-in-arm, into the fair.

CHAPTER 18

THE GREAT OAKS MEDIEVAL FAIRE

As part of the "fun" we were required to dress up in appropriate costumes, but when I saw the old clothes on the rack provided, it gave me the heebie-jeebies. Not only were the costumes old and shabby and probably worn by a hundred people before me, they were all full-length dresses, which made any kind of vampire hunting or parkouring extremely difficult. I had made that mistake before, in the elaborate steel stairwell of the Jupiter Drawing Room, and I wasn't about to make it again. Also, there was no way I was taking my trench coat off, not in this kind of place.

I didn't want to wear the perspiration-perfumed balding velvet on offer, but I knew I had to make some kind of an effort or I'd be denied access. I thought of my nano, but it could only stretch so far. There was one dress on the rail that looked like it could be my style, but I didn't want to get fleas.

Instead, I locked my eyes on the costume I liked the look of and conjured up a clone to fit over my jeans and T-shirt.

"Evoco et excito, nunc et semper, res ac mortales," I whispered under my breath. I stared at the dress and imagined my trench coat turning into a version of it. I felt the fabric grow around me, felt the corset tighten around my waist and push my breasts up. Lace feathered my wrists and ribbons pulled and tightened around me. Extra layers of fabric fell around my legs. I leaned forward and tore off the front section of the skirt so that it wouldn't impede my movement. I inspected the conjured costume in the mirror provided, and it looked good.

I looked around, ready to offer an outfit to Bron, but he popped up in my vision fully dressed as a page boy in navy blue, which suited him well.

We made our way out into the sunshine and the bustling merchants market. There were lines and lines of stalls, which reminded me instantly of EverShade and the Black Magic Market, except that these were friendly and jovial, and didn't make you so scared that you wanted to melt into a puddle on the floor. Gold-crested bunting decorated the Royal Pavilion and tournament ring, which was huge and set in the middle of the sports grounds, and the feast preparations scented the air everywhere we walked.

The merchants were selling everything medieval from hand-crafted jewelry and precious stones to antique furniture, leather everything, live chickens, silks, candles, and gold swords. We reached a stall that was selling ugly clay fairies, dream-catchers, and wands.

Bron stopped and stared at the flair of wands on the table, but I squeezed his shoulders and moved him gently along.

"You don't just *buy* a wand," I whispered in his ear, and he nodded.

I BOUGHT Bron and myself a packet of hot roasted chestnuts from a man with a traveling pot of fire, and we walked around to get the lie of the land, passing the reading tent, the games area, the knighting stone, and Tark's Muddle.

"Now, what do we know about places like this?" I asked Bron. "Nostalgic and quaint?"

"Vampires," he said, crunching his chestnuts.

"Correct." This set-up was a vamp-magnet if I'd ever seen one.

"Is that why we're here?" he asked.

A fire-eater walked past us, stinking of paraffin, and sent a roar of fire out in front of him.

"No," I said. "Although it's tempting."

A short, balding man stepped up onto a box and blew his trumpet to alert us to his forthcoming announcement. He was dressed as a court jester.

"Hear ye, hear ye!" he called in a booming voice in sharp contrast to his stature. "The Great Oaks Medieval Faire is about to begin!"

There was some clapping and cheering from the merchants and a few passers-by.

"Enjoy our fine continuous entertainment, juried crafts and artisans, and foods fit for a king! Celebrate with us in the Brimware Grove. Our shire of Dogwood is filled with outstanding entertainment. Shop for treasures from silks to swords, and hear the pounding of the blacksmith echoing through the misty forest!"

I shuddered at the idea of the misty forest. I think we'd be giving that one a skip.

"Hand-blown glass art, soap-makers and more. Try your hand at archery, axe-throwing and other games of skill. Step back in time to an age of romance and chivalry, where brave knights battle for the favor of the Queen, fair damsels and minstrels frolic, and the villagers enjoy a festival harvest day with much merriment!"

On cue, a minstrel scurried up to the jester and began whistling a cheerful, if not slightly off-key, tune on his flute.

. . .

MY PHONE BEEPED with a message from Isadora. The StarDust Coven was scheduled to meet for tea at the Witches & Wizards Pavilion, just north of the tournament ring, in twenty minutes.

That's a terrible idea, I texted back, but she ignored it, so Bron and I reluctantly made our way over to the shelter, which was decorated with swathes of blue, black and purple fabric, and gold stars. We stopped on the way to watch the visitors try their hand at archery, and my fingers itched to use my brand new crossbow from Ferra, which was clipped to my back. Suddenly I felt a presence behind me, and I whirled around, ready to do battle, but it was just a man, walking with his young family. His face snapped up at my quick movement, and I put up my hand to apologize for startling him. I was seriously on edge. I wanted to get out of there, but we had a job to do.

"We're looking for a witch hunter," I told Bron. "He's already killed one woman, and put another in ICU."

Bron watched as the fair visitors ambled past us, eating fire-roasted turkey legs and frozen custard popsicles. "What does a witch hunter look like?" he asked.

Of course, you can't help picturing *Van Helsing* when you hear the term, but unfortunately for us, I'm sure this man wouldn't make himself so obvious. We scrutinized the people walking by, especially the men walking alone.

"He wouldn't be out in the open like this," I said, and looked in the direction of Brimware Grove, a shaded woodland to the east of the grounds. "Not this one. He's cunning. Calculated."

I had said that Crowe's idea to meet was a terrible one, because it would be flaunting the StarDust Coven members in the open air, essentially making them bait for the hunter. Was that Crowe's plan? To lure the hunter in? Perhaps it wasn't as stupid as I had thought. Reckless, yes. Possibly lethal. But maybe not stupid.

When we reached the Witches & Wizards Pavilion, most of the members were already there. Violet Maleficum, Hazel Shackleton, Erik Tenebris and Paige Periculum were standing in a huddle, discussing something in urgent whispers. When Bron and I walked up to them, they stopped talking and looked at us.

"Don't let me interrupt," I said. Before they had time to reply, Dylan and Ophelia Knox arrived, smiling and waving.

"This fair is wonderful!" said Ophelia, a platter of scones in her hands.

"It's our first time," said Dylan. "We weren't expecting such a show."

Furious-faced Hazel wasn't in the mood for enthusiasm or

cheer. She turned her back on them and faced me. "How is Hettie?"

"Critical." I said. "Stable."

The witches looked relieved and concerned at the same time. Paige's eyes still looked a bit swollen, and I assumed it was from crying the night before. Violet glowered at me, not trusting the stranger in her midst, while Bron continued to crunch away at his chestnuts.

"I have something to tell you," I said. "Something terrible. I think we should sit down."

"But you said Hettie was stable," said Shackleton.

"This isn't about Hettie Frost."

They all looked at me, mouths agape, and I was about to break the news about Fidelis Wolfmoon when I felt a cool hand snake onto my forearm. I turned around to see Isadora Crowe.

"What are you doing here?" I asked.

Crowe pushed her large designer sunglasses up and rested them on the top of her head. Her hair was freshly washed and styled, and her maroon medieval cloak was stunning. Celestine purred happily in the crook of her arm, her just-preened coat matching the rich maroon fabric of the witch's dress.

"Hello Jacquelyn," she said, "hello everybody."

The witches gave her weak smiles, happy to see their high priestess, but anxious to hear what I had to say.

"I didn't know you were coming," I said. "I was just about to tell them—"

Crowe's eyes flashed me a warning. *It's not the time*, her expression said.

"What?" said Violet. "What were you about to tell us?"

"Why don't you help yourselves to tea and scones," said Crowe, gesturing at the refreshment table at the edge of the pavilion covered in a blue satin cloth. "I heard the elderberry jam is particularly good this year. I need a word with Ms. Knight, and will join you in a couple of minutes."

The witches nodded meekly and moved away, and Shackleton stomped after them. There were a few other magical folks around, and when they saw Hazel's face they instinctively moved away from her. She practically radiated fury. Bron didn't need to be told twice. He skipped away from us and joined the coven at the generous platters of scones and clotted cream.

CROW CLAWED my arm and pulled me away to behind the corner of the pavilion, where a wide-trunked climbing wisteria sheltered us from the sun.

"I didn't know you were coming," I said again. "Of course,

you should be the one telling them about Wolfmoon. Which is obviously why you're here."

Isadora looked at me, the shade of the moving leaves of the wisteria dappling her face and adding mystery to her eyes. "I'll tell them, of course," she said. "But only after the *Hexenwald.*"

"What?" I sputtered. "Are you crazy?"

"It's a tradition," said Crowe, firmly. "We do it every year during the Spring Equinox. It's essential to the coven's morale. We need it today more than ever."

"*Filius Canis,* Izzy," I said. "Can't you find another time and place for your bloody team-building?"

Did I have to remind her that there was a killer out there who had an obvious penchant for StarDust witches? Couldn't she plan a paintball match or something, instead of a creepy ritual in a dark forest?

"It's important, Jacquelyn," said Crowe. "We're going through an especially difficult time. The coven is in danger of breaking up. We need to join hands and align our spirits."

"You're crackers," I said. "And I don't mean that in a good way."

"Hazel Shackleton runs the *Hexenwald,*" said Crowe. "Imagine if I took that away from her?"

I saw her point, but I wasn't interested in the coven power play. My job was to keep Crowe alive, and I'd prefer it if we didn't lose any more witches on my watch.

"Let me put it very simply," I said. "If you go through with the *Hexenwald*, I'm off the case."

I was sick of trying to protect people who didn't heed my warnings. If these witches wanted to walk into the dark woods when there was a witch hunter on the loose, then let them. No way I was going in there. My brain bubbled over with all the Latin curse words I could think of.

Isadora looked at me with a pained expression. She bit her lip and shuffled her feet, wasting my time.

"I'm walking away," I said to her, taking a few steps backwards, my hands at my sides. "I'm walking away, Crowe."

"Stop!" she said. "Please. You're right. Of course, you're right. I'll cancel the ritual."

Finally! I thought. *The madness is over.* We could have a scone and get out of there.

I was really thirsty, then, and looking forward to that refreshment table, but then there was a shout from the middle of the grounds, and a loud cry of pain. Crowe put Celestine down and we both started running toward the archery area, where a crowd was gathering. A man—the portly jester—lay on the dry grass, bleeding, clutching the shaft of the arrow buried in his chest.

CHAPTER 19

A KNIGHT IN BURNISHED ARMOR

The man dressed as a court jester lay on his back in the middle of the archery zone, his brass trumpet on the ground beside him. His hands were wrapped around the arrow shaft that protruded from his chest. He was yelling in pain. Isadora elbowed the rubber-neckers out of the way and kneeled down beside him on the dry grass, and I followed. I wondered if we'd have to tag-team a resuscitation again. But as Izzy touched his face, he looked at her and winked. We both stopped, puzzled, until I took a closer look at the arrow shaft, which was not in fact embedded in his ribcage, but stuck on with Halloween magic. Next, a knight in burnished armor arrived, his horse snorting and stamping on the ground, whinnying as he kicked up a low cloud of dust. The knight held a sword.

"Knave!" he shouted across the field, and a ruffian with a bow and quiver cowered against the bales of hay. I looked down at the jester, and smelled the artificial blood. It was the manufactured kind, created for vampires but used for all kinds of things besides, including, apparently, impromptu medieval skits. Crowe and I looked at each other with the same combination of relief and irritation.

It was just a game, I thought. *A set-up.*

But there was still something nagging at me.

A set-up.

And then I felt like someone had shot *me* in the chest, so visceral was my reaction to the realization that this had all been a distraction.

Yesterday I had tried to distract the Hammerskins with an *Aversum* spell, and it didn't seem to work. The witch hunter's magic appeared to be stronger than mine, because both Crowe and I had fallen for this diversion, hook, line and sinker.

"Faex," I said, under my breath, looking up at the Witches & Wizards Pavilion.

"What is it?" asked Crowe, wide-eyed at the way the blood drained from my face.

"We need to get back," I said, gesturing to where we had left the coven dangling like low hanging fruit.

· · ·

Crowe realized, then, too, and her face paled to match mine. We sprinted back in the direction of the pavilion, straight to the refreshment table, but no one from the Star-Dust Coven was there apart from Celestine, the cat, who was lazily grooming her maroon coat. Not for the first time in my life, I wished that animals could talk. Sweet crumbs lay on gold-patterned side plates next to tea-stained cups. The crockery had been stacked neatly, so it didn't look like they had left in a hurry. It seemed to be a deliberate move, a decision, rather than a forced removal. And none of the other witches or wizards milling about looked in the least bit concerned. Well, not until Crowe started yelling.

"Ophelia!" shouted Crowe. "Erik! Violet!"

We searched the veranda and Crowe went to check the restrooms.

I stopped a young man who I recognized from before Isadora had pulled me away. He was drinking coffee and eating a ginger biscuit.

"There was a group of witches here," I said. "Gold glitter on their cloaks."

He frowned and nodded at the same time, then wiped his mouth with a paper serviette. He pointed at the back of the building. "They went that way."

My spine chinked with ice. He was pointing in the direction of the forest.

"Did you see… who… was there anyone with them?" I asked.

He started to shake his head "no," but then changed his mind. "There was someone," he said. "A boy dressed as a page."

MY PHONE BEGAN TO RING, and I grabbed it with trembling fingers.

"Hello?" I asked. My mouth was dry and it felt like all the air had been sucked out of the room.

"Jax," said Morgan. "I think I have something for you."

Crowe reappeared and shook her head. She hadn't found them.

I swallowed hard, trying to force words out. "Tell me."

"You asked me to look into that witch case for you, right?"

"Right," I said, my voice thin.

"Well, we're still looking for other incidences of witches being targeted. We may have something for you there. But something else came up."

"I'm listening," I said.

"Hazel Shackleton. She's a member of the StarDust Coven."

"I know her," I said, picturing the perennially grumpy old hag.

"She has a record."

"What kind of record?" I asked. It's not unusual for someone living on the fringe of society as a witch—or hermit, or mage—to have a criminal record. These people color outside the lines and live by their own ever-shifting moral code rather than the country's rigid set of laws, and conservative cops love to throw their weight around and make their lives difficult.

"A proper criminal record," said Morgan. "It's as long as my arm. Also, she's been in and out of psychiatric institutions since her husband died in—get this—*mysterious circumstances* twenty years ago."

"*Filius Canis,*" I said. "How did he die?"

"Are you ready for this?" Morgan asked.

As ready as I was ever going to be.

"He was found drowned in the bath."

THE PICTURE of Fidelis Wolfmoon was still fresh in my memory, lying with her body and head submerged, staring up at the surface of the water, her wet watch no longer ticking.

Morgan's words echoed in my ears.

Criminal record.

Psychiatric institutions.

Drowned in the bath.

Hazel Shackleton wasn't sojourning in Venice on her leave of absence from the coven, she was being locked up in loony bins. And her sudden appearance with a spade at the Moonlit Chapel had not been a coincidence at all.

I ended the call without saying goodbye or thank you to Morgan.

"Izzy!" I yelled, and Isadora's neck whipped to the side to look at me. "You said Hazel Shackleton was leading the *Hexenwald?*"

"Yes?" she said, looking as terrified as I felt.

"It's her," I said, my voice high. "She's the witch hunter."

And she had Bron.

"It's not possible," said Crowe, frowning and shaking her head. "It can't be."

I had never suspected any of the witches of being the killer, which in retrospect, had been short-sighted. Who else would be let in the house and offered tea? Who else would be close enough to slip a pebble into Crowe's pocket? It was so obvious now it felt like an ice-cold slap in the face. I pulled the crossbow off my back, causing the witches around us to gasp, and we started advancing toward the rear of the hall. I kicked open the door with a loud bang, and together Crowe and I ran into the heavy shade of Brimware Grove.

CHAPTER 20

THE FOREST DARK

Forest witchcraft, and especially rituals like *Hexenwald*, are essential to the modern urban witch. It's easy to get caught up in city life, shopping for pre-made meals at Woolworths and bingeing on Netflix, but the contemporary trappings take their toll on your inherent power. Too many episodes of *Sugar Rush* while you kick back on your *chaise longue* dilute your magic in a slow and insidious way, covering over your core power in gauzy layers until you can no longer feel the pull and glow of it. It feels like your magic is fading, but it's not, it's just being suffocated by modernity.

There is something about forests that bring you back to your magic. It's difficult to explain to untouched people, who can perhaps feel it, but not understand it. There is something in the forest darkness that lights your core. John Berger once said that a forest is what exists between its trees. I know this is true, and every witch knows this is where the magic is.

"Get your wand out," I whispered to Crowe, and she scrambled for it and held it out before her, while my own crossbow zinged with potential magic in my hands. I had to be careful. It was dark under the shade of the canopies and the last thing I wanted to do was shoot the wrong person. My CV is patchy enough as it is. The deep shade was at first welcome and cooling, but as we moved further into the forest it drew my skin out into goosebumps. The tree trunks were gnarled and rough to the touch, and the ground was a carpet of decaying leaves and dry twigs, cracking and snapping as we advanced. Every now and then I scanned the higher branches for vampires, but I saw none.

"Gallanrock," whispered Crowe. "The sacred edifice. They'll be gathered there."

WE TROOPED FURTHER into the dark, and my hands, clutching the crossbow, started to sweat despite the cool of the shadows. I could hear my heart beating, and the adrenaline painted over the pain of my injured eardrum and cracked jaw. Only the smallest shimmers of sun made it through the densely planted trees, and the dappled light flickered like silver butterflies on the forest floor. I kept scanning for vampires, kept sniffing the air for their signature scent, but all I could smell was the leaf mould underfoot.

Crowe stuck out her hand and grabbed my elbow, which gave me such a fright I almost pulled the trigger. She put her finger to her lips, a warning to stay quiet, then looked ahead again, and I followed her stare. In the distance, in the dark, was the sinister silhouette of a person in a cloak who was standing and watching us. Was it Shackleton? I couldn't tell, but my body bristled in fear, telling me all I needed to know. My spine straightened automatically, my muscles clenched. Anxiety squeezed all the breath from my lungs. I had to decide, right then, if I was going to be the hunter or the hunted.

"Shackleton?" I called. The figure didn't move.

I wrenched my arm from Crowe's grip and started sprinting to the silhouette, finger on trigger. I refused to be terrified. Okay, that's not strictly speaking true. I was so scared I felt my bowels liquefy, and my body was covered in a sheen of cold sweat. But to run away would mean more terror, not less, so I ran toward the evil thing, ready to send a bolt into its chest.

"No!" shouted Isadora, but I ignored her. I've always found witches a bit more philosophical, a bit more hands-off, than wizards. I imagined the witch hunter thinking that witches make easy pickings because of their more cautious nature. Well, now there was an armed wizard in the forest, and that evil silhouette's cookies were officially numbered.

But as I gained ground on the cloaked hunter, it disappeared. Right in front of my eyes, one moment it was there, the next it was gone. I stopped to look around, and spent a few seconds with my hands on my knees, recovering my breath. The witch hunter was gone, and when I looked behind me, Crowe was gone, too.

"Izzy?" I shouted. "Izzy!"

The only reply I got was a bird cawing in the distance.

I swore under my breath. Not only had I lost Shackleton, but I'd also lost the whole coven she was targeting. And it's not like I lost them in a safe public place, either, like a shopping mall milkshake bar, or an ice-skating rink. Nope. I managed to lose the whole *deodamn* coven in the middle of the creepiest forest ever, at Spring Equinox, during a medieval fair.

Good work, Jacquelyn Denna Knight. Good freaking work.

I didn't even want to imagine how the debrief with Directress Copperfield would go. My cheeks would have been burning with shame if I didn't have more important things to focus on, like getting the witches out alive. Or getting *most* of them out alive. I had the creeping feeling that the darkness of this forest swallowed people up, and for every dozen that entered, only eleven would return.

I stood still, listening for movement on the brittle-leafed ground, but there was none. Then I heard the bird cawing again, and I realized it was a raven's call. I took a breath and followed the sound. This time I moved slowly; eyes wide, ears pricked up, like a werewolf's. In fact, being a werewolf right then would have some serious advantages, and I considered trying to shift into one, but it would take a lot of magic, and I wasn't sure how much I'd need to battle Shackleton. I had a feeling that the forest would be a lot less scary when experienced in wolverine form. It was tempting, but ultimately too risky. Also, I didn't want to leave my crossbow behind.

I kept moving forward, using the raven's call as a beacon. As I got nearer, I started picking up speed, and I almost tripped over a tree root that was sticking out of the ground, disguised by a mound of leaves. I released the pressure on the trigger just in time to prevent a stray arrow zinging out in front of me. When I recovered from almost falling, armed with an extra spike of adrenaline, I heard the humming of the StarDust Coven's chanting. I recognized it from the night before, at the Moonlit Chapel. A low buzz that practically sparked with magic. And as I got closer still I could feel the forest amplifying the witches' power.

My immediate thought was, *ah, at least they're alive.* But there was a terrible wickedness in the air, which, at first, I thought I was imagining, but it became stronger, the nearer I got. The feeling confused me. I knew the coven was not evil. I knew that Fidelis Wolfmoon was dead and that Hettie Frost was half-dead, and their coven wasn't the reason for either. Was Shackleton, who was leading the powerful forest magic ritual, leading the others into evil? Why would she do that? And was that even possible?

The next raven's caw felt like it was right in my ear, and along with its snapping of wings, it sent my pulse racing. It was a warning, but of what? Bron would know better than to tell me to not approach. Approaching is what I do.

THEN I FELT IT. The vibration through the ground, through my boots and up my legs, into my core. It was getting stronger by the second. I moved closer, and the feeling intensified, as if there was a great magnetic current running right below the earth where I stood. It pulled and pushed me at the same time, and got into my head, as if it meant to short-circuit my brain. The witches' humming got louder and louder, and then just as the feeling was getting to be too much, there was a blast of blue-white light, like a bomb's sudden ripple, and it threw me backwards. I fell and dropped my crossbow. Without missing a beat I used my parkour ground-to-squat jump to get up again and grabbed my weapon. I didn't bother to finger-comb the dead leaves out of my hair. I knew instinctively that something terrible had happened; the knowledge was cold on my skin.

I GRIPPED MY CROSSBOW TIGHTER, but kept my trigger finger light. I saw the stone edifice, then, *Gallanrock*. It was said to have magical powers. A handsome, slate-colored rock the size of a small Japanese car, protruding from the ground at an angle. Twelve surrounding trees bowed over it, their trunks forming a natural birdcage-shaped gazebo. The dappled silver butterflies flitted over the stone itself, adding to its magical allure. I was taken in by the sight even though I was on high alert after the raven's warning, and I stared at the rock for a full ten seconds before I noticed the bodies lying all around it on the ground.

CHAPTER 21

AIR

Eight witches lay motionless on the dry leaves, the angle of their bodies radiating out from the chalk-circle cast around the base of the rock, their heads at the roots of the bowing trees. Aware that the hunter was most likely in my midst, I crept slowly up to one of them—Violet—and felt for a pulse. As I touched the pads of my fingers to her slender wrist her eyes clicked open, and they were black and wet as they were the night before, at the haunted chapel, and I flinched and moved away, almost falling backwards onto another body. It was Ophelia Knox, and her eyes were the same at Violet's. I looked at the rest of the witches splayed in the circle, as pale as corpses, and demonic-looking with their bottomless ink eyes. I felt almost weightless with fright, as if I would faint, or run in the air, but then the math brought me back to earth.

Twelve trees.

Eight witches.

Hettie was in critical care, Wolfmoon in the morgue. I spotted Paige, Dylan Knox and Erik Tenebris on the ground, and did a quick scan of the other witches. Apart from Crowe, only one was missing. I inhaled a long, slow breath. Hazel Shackleton.

Hazel Shackleton, the furious old crone with a penchant for drowning husbands and other annoying creatures. Why didn't I see it earlier? Perhaps because I didn't want to see it. Didn't want to believe that it was one of the coven's own members who would terrify them like this. Although, to be frank, they were the ones who were terrifying me at that moment.

Standing inside the organic gazebo, I heard something move behind me in the forest and I jumped and turned around, grappling to get a good grip on my crossbow. I searched, but I saw no one.

"Come out, Hazel," I said, my voice gruff with nerves. "Come out and you won't get hurt."

Silence.

"Come out, Shackleton," I called again.

This time the snapping sound came from the direction of the edifice, and I spun so quickly the forest blurred, and I yelled in fright at what I saw.

Hanging from the central point, where the twelve trees met at the top of the cage, was a rope tied into a noose, and Hazel Shackleton's bulging, purple-faced body hung from it, dangling above the *Gallanrock*.

THAT IMAGE WILL STAY with me always. The magical setting turned malefic. Hazel's fury finally snatched away from her, leaving her meek and mild looking, arms hanging by her side in her witch's cloak, so faded that it was a dark shade of gray. The shifting sunrays highlighting her body as it swayed ever so slightly.

"Help!" I shouted, without thinking. Without worrying that the killer was probably right there in the shadows. "Help!" My voice woke up some of the witches, and they began to stir. I clipped my crossbow to my back and climbed up onto the rock with my dirty boots—its sacred magic be damned —and tried to push Hazel up to release the pressure on her neck. Her body was totally limp. Once I had a grip on her, I shouted *"Ignem Exquiris!"*

The fear in my body focused into a white laser, which I used to cut the rope just above her head, and I tumbled to the ground with Hazel, smacking my elbow on the rock on the way down and sending blue sparks of pain up my arm.

"What?" someone behind me asked.

"What's going on?" said another voice.

Then there were gasps of shock and mournful moaning.

Once we were on the ground, I straddled Shackleton and wrestled with the noose around her neck, tried to loosen it, but as I was doing so I knew I was too late. The way her head lolled on the floor told me her neck was broken. I fought to remove the rope anyway, I couldn't stand it coiled around her throat like that, and eventually I got it off and threw it onto the ground beside us.

Someone was standing at my shoulder. I turned to see a pale-lipped Isadora Crowe, who looked at me with a grim expression. I was sitting astride the body, and could feel something small and hard underneath my right thigh. I stood up, shaking, and checked Hazel's pocket for the adder stone I knew would be there.

It was a pretty one; smooth in my palm, ivory colored and engraved with the elemental symbol for *air*. I looked up at Crowe again. We both knew she would be next.

CHAPTER 22

BLEEDING AT LEISURE

I escorted the shell-shocked coven out of the forest, armed with my crossbow and a fierce feeling of dread. Crowe settled them at the pavilion, made them hot sweet tea and told them everything she knew. Their faces were stamped with shock and as white as the sugar Crowe loaded into their tea. They didn't remember chanting, they said. They didn't remember anything but gathering around *Gallanrock* and holding hands, ready to begin the forest magic ritual. Ophelia Knox was crying, saying it was her fault. She was the one who urged the rest into the forest. It was going to be the Knox couples' first *Hexenwald*, and she had been so looking forward to it. She hadn't known it would be dangerous. Dylan, her husband, held her tenderly and comforted her.

"It's going to be okay," he whispered into her hair, and kissed her head.

Isadora Crowe was the palest of them all. She may as well have had the fingerprints of the grim reaper all over her; so clearly marked was her fate. Even Celestine seemed spooked. I made her promise to meet me at my apartment the minute she finished debriefing the coven. I wasn't sure I could protect her, but without me she was a sitting duck. I took her assistant, Paige, aside, and told her the same thing.

"*Make sure she comes straight to my place,*" I had said, and she nodded.

I called Morgan, but she wasn't available, so I logged the incident with the Scorpion receptionist instead, who said she'd send a team out right away.

Bron was nowhere to be seen, which worried me. Had he followed the witch hunter? Or had something worse happened? I didn't want to think about it, but the anxiety clawed at my stomach. *My Kresnik will come back to me,* I told myself. *He'll find me.*

I biked back to my apartment feeling supremely on edge. Usually the ride comforts me, but my nerves were buzzing so loudly in my ears that I could hardly think. Every bird in the sky made me do a double-take. I hoped like hell that Bron would already be home, safe and sound, and ready to tell me what he had seen at *Gallanrock,* but somehow I knew that life—or at least *my life*—didn't seem to work out quite as neatly as that.

. . .

Case in point: there was blood smeared on my front door when I arrived home, and Gnor was awake, for once, and wide-eyed. I frowned at the stain and then at my orc security guard.

"Bron home?" I asked him. "The boy raven?"

Gnor shook his head. "Woman."

With the rest of the StarDust Coven either dead, in the hospital or back at the medieval fair, I couldn't guess which woman would be bleeding at leisure in my apartment.

"Hello?" I called, pushing the door open. There was a streak of blood on the wall, and drops on the floor. I entered cautiously, in case it was a trap. The Void knows I had already fallen prey to one distraction today, and it had proven fatal—to Hazel Shackleton.

The picture of her hanging limp flashed in my mind, as I knew it would. I'd have to get used to that image; I was going to live with it forever.

"Hello?" I said again, and walked through a cold patch of air that made my breath turn white. Ghost was there, and he didn't seem frantic, so I took that as a good sign. I didn't have to venture far to find the source of my apartment's new color scheme.

Lou, the neighborhood drug dealer, was slumped over in my charity shop chair.

"Holy *faex*!" I said, "Are you all right?"

Lou looked up at me. Her quinine eye was fused shut, her nose was broken. Her lip was split in more than one place and her whole face was freshly bruised and swollen, hazelnut skin turned cruel navy blue.

"What the hell happened?" I asked. "Who did this to you?"

When Lou spoke, I saw that one of her front teeth was chipped.

"Give you one guess," she said, and winced, grabbing her torso. "They caught me off-guard. If I had seen them coming, I would have been able to protect myself."

She winced in pain.

"Broken rib?" I asked.

"Probably."

I ran to get the new first aid kit I had bought at *Mason & Sons*, quickly checking on Darick on the way. He seemed healed now, but still he slept. Was something else wrong? Was I missing something? Gizmo looked happy, curled up and sleeping on his broad chest.

"I'm no doctor," I said to Lou when I returned with the case.

"I assumed as much," she said.

I knelt down on the injured Mona Lisa pillow and opened the steel case, relieved to find the stacks of clean white cotton pads, bandages, plasters, and bright antiseptic liquid inside.

"Your timing is bad," I said.

"Next time I'll plan to get beaten up at a more convenient time," snarked Lou.

"I just meant that... do you remember the stalker that used to hang around? You warned me about him."

"I haven't seen him stalk you in a while," she said. "Good riddance."

"Actually, he's in my bedroom."

Lou exclaimed in pain as I applied the antiseptic-soaked pad to her grazed forehead and cheek.

"Funny one," she said, then grimaced and held her ribcage again.

"Not kidding," I replied. I worked slowly, attending to the smaller lacerations before taking on the more serious looking ones. I wouldn't be able to do anything about her broken bones. I could try to heal them, but I didn't like the odds of it working. I was notoriously bad at mending things in general, plus I didn't have my wand to concentrate and focus my power. If only Darick was awake.

"I told you to be careful of him," said Lou.

"He saved my life."

"So he's charming, I get it."

"No, he literally saved my life. I was dying on the floor and he fixed me. He found the bullet in my chest and stitched me up with nothing but his hands. I said your timing was off because if he was conscious, he could fix you, too. He's a mage with healing powers."

"You've got an unconscious healer mage in your bedroom?"

"Yes," I said, even though I didn't think it was really a question.

I gingerly started on her swollen-shut eye, but she flinched and held up her hand. "Leave it," she said. "Please."

I saw then that her knuckles were cut and bruised, too, and I wasn't surprised. I imagined her as a fighter. I reached into my trench coat pocket and retrieved the gift from the old fossil at the magical apothecary. *Healing Salve*, the tin said. I applied it to Lou's worst cuts and gave the rest to her to keep.

"Don't think we're even, now," she said, and then added "Ha," but didn't laugh, I guessed on account of her fractured ribcage.

"You'll need to see someone," I said. "About the broken bones."

"I know someone who can sort it out," she said. "But my broken bones are the least of our problems," she said.

"*Our* problems?"

She looked at me, her skin shining with the ointment. "I'm not here for your nursing skills."

"Am I that bad?" I asked. I had this new first aid kit and everything. I was actually pretty impressed with my work.

"Don't get me wrong," she said. "I'm grateful for the help. But that's not why I'm here."

CHAPTER 23
IT'S YOUR FUNERAL

"They were looking for *you*," said Lou.

"What?" I asked.

Lou gestured vaguely at the damage to her face. "They were looking for you."

"No," I said, in disbelief. "The people who did this to you?"

"The *Hammerskins* who did this to me," she said, and I saw her struggle to swallow.

"Oh no," I said, lamely. I couldn't think of anything else to say. "Oh no, I'm so sorry."

I felt instantly sick. Guilt and fear hardened everything inside me, making my stomach cramp.

"They know you live here, in this building. They don't know which number, or which floor. I wouldn't tell them."

"Thank you," I said. "I'm so sorry."

"I don't want to hear that one more time," she said, looking straight at me, her swollen eye making me feel guiltier still. "You are not responsible for the actions of a bunch of Neo-Nazi orcs."

"I know, but—"

"But, nothing," she said. "Stop apologizing. Start thinking."

"Thinking? Of what?"

"Of how to get out of here without them seeing you. About how to protect yourself when they find you, because *they will find you*. You need to plan where you'll stay in the meantime."

"I'm not staying anywhere!" I said. "They won't force me out of my own home."

Besides, Crowe was on her way here. We had a deal. I needed to protect her.

Lou pulled a face, then winced accordingly. She gritted her teeth. "You don't get it. *They are psychopaths. They are coming after you.*"

I felt hot and cold at the same time, as if I were coming down with the flu, and my skin felt fevered. "I don't have anywhere to go."

"It won't be forever," Lou said, more gently. "Just till—"

"Till when?" I said. "That's the problem. The Hammerskins aren't going anywhere."

Lou crossed her arms, broken ribs and all. "I don't know what else to say."

I thought of Ghost, and Darick. And Crowe, who should have been there by then.

"Thank you for the warning, but I'm not going to run from a bunch of thug skinheads. I'd rather stay, and fight."

I had my crossbow, and people to protect. Besides, there were eleventy hundred floors in that skyscraper. It would take them weeks to knock on every door. Unless they started at the top, in which case, I'd better feed Gnor caffeine tablets and nail my front door shut, pronto.

"Fine, I get it," Lou said. She stood up with a bleak expression on her face. And pulled her hoodie on, hissing with pain as she did so. "It's your funeral."

"Let's hope that remains a figure of speech," I said.

"Ha," she said again, shuffling toward the door.

As she reached the doorway she turned around slowly. "Oh," she said. "Before I forget." She reached into the leather bag she keeps strapped to her hips and pulled out a small vial of the brightest blue I'd ever seen. She looked at it and lobbed it to me, and I caught it with both hands.

"Venom," she said, as it sparkled in my palm. "You said you wanted some."

"You said you didn't sell it."

"Yes, well, the Hammerskins had other ideas."

"What?" I said, my brain whirring. "What do the Hammerskins have to do with Venom?"

Lou pursed her split lip. "Seems that they're the distributors. They said if I didn't want to be a supplier, they'll replace me with someone who will. And when they said *replace,* I don't think they were talking about finding me another post."

AFTER LOU LEFT, I paced my apartment floor, which is trickier than it sounds, seeing as my entire square meterage is roughly the size of a postage stamp. After our street brawl, I knew the Hammerskins were going to come after me, I just didn't expect them to find my building so quickly. A part of me was desperate to run, but I knew that wherever I chose would not be safe for long. Anyway, where would I go? Would I just show up at the Khargol Isles to surprise the pregnant pickle in a bikini, Sugar Shagar? Or to London, from where I'd received a postcard from Estelar Pavaris, who had moved there with his new lover and joined the Royal Theatre?

· · ·

My stomach was still twisting in on itself after what Lou had told me, and I felt my darkness rise up inside me. Guilt, terror, and dread threatened to overwhelm me. I put my head down and walked into the kitchen to make a cup of tea, and as I moved to fill the kettle with water I saw that my plant had not only survived losing its pot, but also the attack I had launched on it, cutting it all the way down to a slip. I had been tempted to throw that slip away, but it was too useful of an indicator as to how the vampire pocket realm was faring. It had been a mere hint of a plant after I had chopped it back last night, but it had already grown new leaves and coiling stems and suckers to replace every branch I had cut off. Not only had it grown back, but it seemed stronger than before, and had... evolved? I could swear the thing didn't have those suckers before, and its leaves seemed thicker, less destructible. I shuddered. It was a scary idea that by cutting it back I had just made it stronger. What did that mean for the Silvano Clan, and what did that mean for the Realm?

Suffice to say I skipped the tea and opened a bottle of Ferra's cinnamon whisky instead. I grabbed a scuffed tumbler from a cupboard that hadn't yet been colonized by the invasive vine, and poured myself a double shot. I drank it while I stared at the plant, thinking. The whisky did nothing to dissolve the darkness.

I dragged my eyes to the small vial of Venom on my kitchen counter. It was really the most incredible tint of blue. And it wasn't a flat color, but shimmered and changed shades in flickers of cerulean and sapphire. I could tell just by looking at it that it was more of a potion than a hard drug. No wonder it had looked so strange under the microscope when we compared it to other non-magical drugs. I had to figure out why the Hammerskins were distributing it, and why they were trying to feed untouched humans a newly designed potion that no one had ever heard of. I wondered briefly if I should tell the Council, but then I remembered that they hadn't responded to any of my previous hotline messages, which added to my 99 problems. Because if the Council wasn't functioning properly... well, we were all in for a world of pain. I took my phone out of my pocket, considering sending them another alert, but then saw a missed call from Izzy.

Faex! She must have tried to phone me when I was busy with Lou. I tried to call her back, but her phone was off. I took a deep breath and tried not to let my nerves get the better of me. She was probably just calling to say she was on her way. Or that her battery was running low. Or both. What was taking so long?

CHAPTER 24

A COLD HURRICANE

I paced some more and drank some more, then repeated the ritual while I felt the pull of the vial of Venom on my kitchen counter, which was glowing at me in azure, cobalt and cyan with sparks of silver. I wondered if I needed to go out to find Crowe, but with the Hammerskins camped outside, I knew that it would be reckless. She promised she would come as soon as the coven was safe and settled, and the police were finished with their report. Perhaps that was what was taking so long. There would be a lot of questions about how Shackleton died, especially after Wolfmoon's death that morning, and Frost's attempted murder the night before. In fact, the cops had probably shut that medieval fair down mid-feast with all its honey mead and succulent turkey legs and made sure that no one got out of there without a thorough interrogation.

Without even trying, I had made my way through a third of the bottle of Copper Cog whisky, and it made me miss Ferra like crazy. No matter what, I decided, I'd make time to see her the next day. Ferra always seemed to be able to settle the dark stuff inside me. She'd feed me a golden pot pie—beef and stout, perhaps—with gravy, and spiced pumpkin, and a good cold lager, and she'd punch me on the arm, and I'd see her ruffle the hair of one of her dozen kids, and everything would feel better again.

Just get through tonight, I told myself. *Everything will seem better in the morning.*

Sometimes I'm an expert at lying to myself, but at other times I know better. Nothing would be improved in the morning. If anything, it would be worse. The plant would have doubled in size, the witch hunter would be zeroing in on Crowe, and the Hammerskins would find me, *sans* wand, and probably with a mean hangover. Darick would still be hibernating, Salty and Bron would still be missing, and Lou would still be in pain. And my darkness would still be swirling around me like it was then, like a black mist, a cold hurricane trying to vacuum out my heart.

Something came over me, a despair that I can only remember feeling when I was sleeping out on the winter streets with an empty belly and no promise of food in sight. A cold deep-bone ache. I tried to fight it, but it was strong. I felt as if it was pushing me to the floor, but I would not be laid low by it.

Pictures of my parents, alive and smiling in childhood memories, and then dead in their bed, came to me. Also, the memory of what it felt like to lie dying on the Khargol carpet while Qwynkle's crazy bullet wrecked my insides. The pool of blood, the pain. Almost choking to death in Slyden Abarim's enchanted basement, surrounded by hungry, squeaking rats. Liz Durison's branded corpse. Hettie Frost's fingers, worn to the bone trying to scratch her way out of the coffin. And Hazel Shackleton, hanging from that noose.

I felt like I was going insane, like my mind was trying to tell me something, or torture me, or both, and I pressed my palms up against my temples and whispered for it to stop.

Please stop, I said. *I can't stand it. Please stop.*

There was silence for a moment, and peace, and then my eyes were drawn to the vial on the counter again. It was the most beautiful potion I had ever seen. I thought then that I should try it on myself. If I knew how the drug worked and felt, I would have a better understanding of it. Sure, it was a little dangerous. I had already seen how the untouched people had reacted when they tried it. They just disappeared for a little while for their mini-Rapture vacation and came straight back to their regular lives, right? Well, what if I could somehow remember where I went in that time, and use that knowledge to help Morgan solve the case? The Void knows I owe that woman a favor, after all she'd done for me, and after all the waiting around on the V-Cult case she'd been doing while I was blithely solving all the other cases around it. The more I thought about it, the less crazy the idea seemed.

But you've had a bit to drink, I cautioned, eyeing the well-dented whisky bottle.

You shouldn't make this kind of decision on a bellyful of Ferra's delicious home-distilled cinnamon-bark-barreled whisky.

And you certainly shouldn't mix potions with alcohol.

You learn that in *Potions 101*, and they remind you of it every year should you not have been paying attention in class that first time around, dreaming of finding the owl hiding in the robes of the copper statue of Minerva, or the white crayon lying on your windowsill.

I moved closer to the counter and watched the potion flicker like the eye of an ice dragon. It was powerful and mesmerizing. Those muggles wouldn't stand a chance resisting it. I picked it up and screwed the lid off. It even smelled delicious, which potions seldom do. Vanilla vodka with silver sparks of effervescence. I would have just a tiny bit, not even half a dose. I'd leave plenty for the next day, when I'd take it to *Mason & Sons* and ask them to use their potion spinner to deconstruct and analyze it. I lifted the vial to my lips. I'd just put a drop on my tongue, and leave the rest.

You're making a mistake, the voice inside my head said, but the self-destructive darkness pushed it away. Ghost hit me with a cold gale, making the hairs on the back of my neck stand up, then slammed the red hardcover onto the floor with a bang that echoed through my too-quiet apartment.

THE VENOM TASTED JUST like its sweet-sparking aroma, and the drop of cool liquid felt good on my tongue. I resisted the urge to finish it off, and put the vial back on the counter with a steady hand. A low, beautiful buzz started at the base of my neck and traveled up and over my skull. My lips tingled, and my vision softened. All of a sudden my apartment looked quite cozy, where before it was grim and stark and cold. The buzz didn't stop at my head, but traveled down my body, arching my spine and settling in my pelvis. It was an amazing sensation; so warm, and so wonderful. I felt as if my whole body was pulsing with color, and I thought I'd go and lie down next to Darick and just enjoy the feeling, relax into the relief of it. My muscles had been so stiff before, my nerves stretched so taut, but now I was glowing with wellness.

I pulled out my phone—still no message from Crowe—and recorded a voice message to myself to document what I might not remember after the drug wore off.

"Two minutes in, and it feels freaking amazing. Everything about the Venom is delicious. My body is on, like, a slow-burn to pleasure. I'm assuming it's highly addictive. No magical effects experienced yet."

What I didn't say is that I was feeling pretty turned on, too. I remembered the moment Darick and I shared, before he was hurt. We were in my bedroom, and I was freshly showered and just wearing a towel. I thought of his broad chest, his perfect skin, so unlike mine, which is a map of battle scars. I had dropped the towel anyway.

THE DOORBELL RANG, startling me, and shaking me out of the daydream.

Finally! Crowe.

I quickly hid the vial of Venom in my cutlery drawer and banged it shut with my hip. She'd probably judge me for being as high as a kite but I didn't give a *faex.* I rushed to the door and opened it, but there was no one there, and Gnor was drooling in his sleep.

"Hello?" I said. "Izzy? Bron?"

I stepped out into the warm night air and looked around.

"Ms. Knight," said a voice from the shadows. A vampire's voice, one that I recognized. He stepped out into the light, looking like a Swedish supermodel with his perfectly styled blond hair and notorious cheekbones.

"Lysander," I said. "I heard you have something for me."

"May I come in?" he asked.

"Since when do you need an invitation?"

He smiled. "I don't want to intrude."

I almost laughed. "Usually I put an arrow through the hearts of any vampires that show up here."

"I know," he said. "I was hoping you'd skip that part of the reception."

I looked at him while I tapped my boot on the floor, wrestling with the truth, which was that I actually did want him to come in. What the hell was wrong with me? Had the darkness finally overwhelmed me, or was it the drug speaking? Either way, I gestured with a flick of my head that the vampire could enter, and as he brushed past me to go inside, it felt good.

CHAPTER 25

HONEYED HAZE

"I like what you've done with the place," joked Lysander. I frowned at him, not sure what he meant, and he motioned at the smears of blood on the wall. They had all but disappeared in my haze of awesomeness.

"Whisky?" I said, holding up the bottle. The label looked beautiful in the evening light, as the copper cog and lever illustrations on the cream paper whirred away. I got lost in the animation for a minute. Lysander seemed surprised that I was staring at a label and offering him a drink, instead of pointing my crossbow at his chest.

"Are you okay?" he asked.

"Peachy!" I said. I don't know why I said *peachy*. I've never once in my life used the word *peachy*. I wasn't even one hundred percent sure I knew what the word meant. I mean, I knew what it meant, but I didn't know why. My thoughts rambled on to envision golden orchards brimming with bright blushing peaches, fresh with dew. I could practically taste the sweet white flesh in my mouth.

Deodamnatus, that Venom was powerful stuff.

If this is what one drop feels like, how much would I be tripping on a whole dose?

It was very tempting to find out. I fought the urge, and instead looked down at the counter, ready to pour the vampire a drink, but I found I had already done so. Two tumblers stood, waiting, and I had no memory of pouring them. I passed one to Lysander, who thanked me, and was still looking at me strangely.

"There's something wrong," he said. "I can see it."

"Believe me, there is a lot wrong," I said. "Everything is wrong." But my body had other ideas. My body thought that everything felt very right. The drug was still kicking in. I felt waves of pleasure flowing through me. It was all I could do to not stop and groan in pleasure.

"Everything is wrong," I said again. "Can't you see it?"

After all, there we were, a vampire and a vampire-slayer, and not a stake in sight.

"No," he said. "I think everything is going according to plan."

"Of course you do." I should have felt angry with him, then, but instead I found that my body was drawn to him, and I moved closer without wanting or meaning to.

"You have something for me," I said.

Lysander took a sip of his drink and put the glass down carefully on the counter. Usually my tumblers are chipped and scuffed, but through the filter of the drug they looked like polished crystal. I watched as the amber liquid in his glass finished rippling, watched it until it was as still as Fidelis Wolfmoon's bathwater, then I looked up at Lysander again, who was staring at me with an intense look on his face.

Where were we?

I kept getting lost in the small moments.

"You're drunk?" he asked.

I shook my head. "Not drunk." Then changed it to: "Okay, a little bit drunk."

On top of being *a little bit drunk*, I was clearly insane, too, admitting vulnerability to a vampire that belonged to the most vicious clan in the Realm. The frightening thing is that I was opening myself up to being taken advantage of. The more frightening thing was that a part of me *wanted* to be taken advantage of. Given my troubled past and my burning hatred of vampires, this thought alone should have made me feel acutely uncomfortable, but I felt more comfortable in my skin at that moment than I had ever felt before in my life. I could have been naked right then, standing right there, and I wouldn't have felt self-conscious in the slightest. Speaking of which, it was getting pretty warm, so I took off my trench coat and undid a couple of buttons on my shirt. All the problems I had which had seemed so crushing an hour before, so suffocating, now felt manageable. To add to my sense of fortune, Lysander reached under his cape and brought out my mother's silver wand.

It was so good to see it again, it felt so right. I was about to reach for it when I realized it wouldn't be as easy as that. The wand was leverage for Lysander. There'd be a deal to be made.

"Tell me what you want," I said.

There's no such thing as a free lunch, especially when there's a vampire involved.

"I want a lot of things," he said, and I could hear him breathing, could see the rise and fall of his chest that was so close to me. My own body was still radiating color and pleasure.

I swallowed a sip of whisky. "Can you be more specific?"

Lysander handed me the wand. Or, rather, he held it out to me, and it jumped on its own accord into my palm, and it felt right.

"What?" I said, "No *quid pro quo*?"

"A *thank you* will suffice."

"I don't believe you," I said. "Everything in your world comes at a price."

"And what about your world?" he asked.

"We do favors for each other without wondering what it'll cost us down the line."

This wasn't true, strictly speaking, but I was going to run with it.

"Well," he said, "this won't cost you anything."

Somehow I found that difficult to believe, but my gratitude toward him was real.

"Thank you," I said, and we stared into each other's eyes for a moment.

My body was buzzing, my pelvis throbbing. I was back in my bedroom, standing with Darick, water droplets still on my skin. Expecting Darick to kiss me hard and deep, I angled my face backwards, ready for him, wanting him. But then Darick's face disappeared and Lysander was there, his arm around my back, his face close to mine—too close—but I didn't move away. I wanted him to touch me. My body demanded it. Blond hair turned to brown again and I looked into Darick's face and saw my burning desire reflected in his eyes. My body was throbbing with the urgency of it. I felt his lips brush my cheek and my insides felt like they were opening up to him, a tight crimson bud blooming into a flower, pushing its petals outwards and reveling in finally realizing its potential. I moved closer to him, pushing my pelvis into his and embracing the warmth I found there, which amplified the thrilling buzz of the Venom.

Darick. Lysander. Darick. My urgent desire could no longer tell them apart. Through the honeyed haze of the drug, they became one person. I needed this.

Lysander.

His arm tightened around me, cinnamon on his breath. My body buckled under my desire, and he took my weight. I thought of the mesmerizing appearance of the Venom, the silver sparks, which I felt now all over my skin.

Darick. We were meant to be together. I felt so safe in his arms.

I dropped the towel, angled my head, and waited for the deep, hungry kiss. I was so ramped up, then, I was ready to explode into stars. Lysander moved his lips toward mine. That's when I turned my face slightly, and offered him my neck.

"Bite me," I said, and I felt Lysander's body press against mine, and our bodies burned where they touched. Our breathing was deep and full of desperate longing. I moved closer to him still. His lips were on my neck, feather-light, sending an intense thrill right through my body. I'd never felt anything like that before and I groaned hard, and he did, too.

"Bite me," I said, the words sounding terrible, and right, at the same time. I didn't care. All I wanted were Lysander's fangs buried in my neck.

CHAPTER 26

BAYONETS FRESHLY SHARPENED

"Jacquelyn," he said, and I opened my eyes. "Jacquelyn!"

I felt like I was waking up. Lysander held me in his arms as if we were at the end of a dance.

A headache rushed into my skull like an advancing army, bayonets freshly sharpened. My mouth was a nightclub ashtray, my fingers numb. The Venom had worn off almost instantly, and with a vengeance. The come-down was brutal.

"What?" I said. "What happened?"

He lifted my body in his arms and walked me across the room, placing me gently in the chair, then crouched down on his haunches to look at me and feel my forehead. I don't know what he was feeling for. Proof of insanity, maybe. A psychological break.

"What happened?" I asked again. I wished that I had absolutely no recollection of what had just occurred, but the hard-to-swallow truth was that I remembered everything. Or almost everything. I remembered enough to make my cheeks burn with an emotion more destructive than shame. I had betrayed Darick, and the memory of my parents. I had betrayed every innocent person killed by a vampire, and the grief-stricken people they left behind. Most guttingly, I had betrayed myself. I was so shocked and disgusted by it that I retched right there. I felt too sick to cry.

"You're ill," Lysander said. "You fainted. I knew it. You haven't... been yourself."

My face fell into my hands. I felt dizzy, and too weak to hold my head up straight. "Venom," I mumbled.

"What?"

"Venom," I said again, but then I had to dart from the room. Lysander sensed where I was going and moved with me, just in time to hold my hair back as I emptied my worried stomach's contents into the old stained toilet bowl in my bathroom.

I groaned and flushed the vile stuff away, wishing I could do the same with the evening's memories. I moved to the basin and rinsed my face and mouth, then buried my head in a balding towel. When I looked up, Lysander was still there, a concerned expression on his face.

"Why are you still here?" I asked him, under the unflattering light of the bare, buzzing bulb.

"Tell me what's wrong with you," he said.

"It's not me," I said. "I would never—"

"I know," Lysander said.

I rubbed my eyes and replaced the towel on the grimy hook. I limped into the kitchen, my whole body dragging from the dissipation of the drug. I opened the kitchen drawer and took out the half-full vial, held it up to the light so that he could see it.

"What's that?" he asked.

"They call it Venom."

A shadow winged across his face. "You shouldn't have that," he said. "Where did you get it?"

"So you know about it," I said.

Even in my overcast thoughts, I found that interesting. Now, why would a vampire know about a magical drug designed for muggles, distributed by orc Neo-Nazis? What had Venom to do with vampires?

"You," I said. "You did this."

He shook his head. "No. This has nothing to do with me."

"You did this," I said again, louder. My voice reverberated in my flaming skull.

"Give it to me," he said. "Let me get rid of it."

I clasped the vial tightly and held it to my chest. "No."

Lysander set his handsome jaw. "Jacquelyn," he said. "You were never supposed to have it. Never mind drink the stuff."

"I wish I hadn't!" I yelled. That was the truth. The other, more disturbing truth was that I wanted more. I wanted to finish the bottle. My body was aching for it. The rational, responsible side of me knew I needed what was left in the vial to take to the magical apothecary. It was our only chance of finding out what it was and where it was coming from. I also knew that as soon as Lysander left I'd gulp down the remainder of the potion whether I decided to, or not.

LYSANDER HAD READ MY THOUGHTS, and he lunged for the vial, inadvertently smacking me down to the floor and landing on top of me, winding me so that my chest burned for air. My lips opened, trying to drag oxygen into my shocked lungs, and Lysander's face was so close to mine I thought he might try to kiss me. Then I realized the vial had been knocked from my hand, and lay shattered on the cheap kitchen tiles. My fury was a white hot flame.

"*Fiat Fulgar!*" I yelled, breathlessly, and the pain in my temples flew down my body and through my arms. The lightning spell shot through Lysander's shoulders and blew his body off mine. He gasped in pain and shock.

I jumped up in my parkour move, floor-to-haunches, and glared at him.

"Get out," I said, but he didn't move. The expression on his face told me he couldn't believe that after what we had been through, I would send a current through him. But that was because he didn't know me. I spotted my wand on the kitchen counter and put my hand out to it. The wand bee-lined straight into my palm, like a magnet finding its mate. I pointed the wand at Lysander.

"Get out," I said again.

He narrowed his eyes at me, glancing down at the wand in my trembling hand. "You wouldn't."

"You think you know me," I said, trying to keep my voice even. "You think just because you have my file from a million years ago that you know me."

My wand sparked, and he took a step back.

"I'm not that little girl anymore," I said, gruff, and shudder-ing. "I'm not that orphan wizard you read about. I'm past that. I'm more than that."

"I know," said Lysander. "I can feel your power. I felt it from the beginning."

We stared at each other. We had a connection whether we liked it or not.

I wiped my mouth with the back of my hand. "I'm giving you one more chance to leave."

"I didn't mean to take advantage of you," he said. "I didn't know you were on Venom or I wouldn't have come."

"Ha," I said, the bitter laugh hanging in the air between us. "You think *you* took advantage of *me*?"

My wand sent a small bolt in his direction, too short to hurt him but just long enough to get him moving. He put his hands up in surrender.

"I'm going," he said.

"You should never have come," I replied.

CHAPTER 27
VAMPIRE VENOM

The withdrawal from even half a dose of Venom is not pretty. My body felt like it was shrinking from the inside. As if someone had attached my feet to one of those FreshSaver vacuum-pack machines and was sucking the life out of me, sucking out my will to live. There was a dagger in my brain, and my joints ached like a geriatric after a rock 'n roll concert. I tried to siphon some of the blue liquid up off my grimy kitchen floor, thinking that even a milliliter might help, but the potion had evaporated. I got the brush and pan instead, and swept up the shattered glass, cursing Lysander with every shard.

My betrayal of everything and everyone hurt more than the physical withdrawal. It hurt me so deep down that I didn't think I'd ever be able to ease the feeling. I still couldn't believe what had happened. I had been under a spell.

I sat down on the cool tiles and leaned up against a cabinet door, studying the contents of the cracked plastic pan. I picked up the small black screw-top lid, which was still attached to a glass shard, and closed my eyes. I had never been suicidal before, never, even on the coldest, darkest days on the street, still freshly keening for my parents. I had never wanted to end my life and I didn't want to now, either, but I was somehow tempted to press the broken glass against my pale wrists. It was the darkness inside me urging it. The drug had painted over the desperation, but paint bubbles and chips away, and now the darkness was back, colder and more menacing than ever.

Damn you, Lysander, I thought, dropping the lid of the vial back into the pan. Even though, strictly speaking, the man had done nothing wrong. Or at least, nothing wrong while he had been here in my apartment. He had brought my wand back, with no conditions attached. He had held my hair back as I had ralphed unceremoniously and with great gusto into the ceramic bowl. He had tried to protect me from myself. Most importantly, he hadn't bitten me when I had urged him to, even though we had both wanted it so badly at the time.

Two things came to me then, two new ideas that sparked some hope in my otherwise shadow-struck mind. The first was that Lysander had known what the drug was, so I could surmise that the vicious vampire clan he belonged to had a hand in this new magical drug scourge. I also remembered Morgan saying that criminal reports of vampire attacks on untouched humans was down. I knew that the vampires were growing in power and recklessness, so I was pretty sure that they were not scaling back on attacks. The humans were just *reporting* it less.

Why would they fail to report? I asked myself, and for once, I knew the answer. I had just been through it myself. The drug-addled humans weren't reporting the vampire attacks because they thought they *wanted it to happen*. Something in the potion, by evil-genius design, made you *want* to be bitten by a vampire. It wasn't just Venom, it was Vampire Venom.

Although my cheeks burned, I forced myself to relive the hot encounter I'd just experienced with Lysander. In that moment, every fiber of my being was screaming to be touched by the vampire, but not just touched. I craved urgently the feeling of his fangs buried in my neck. I felt that if he just sunk his teeth into me and sucked, that it would make me explode in a thousand silver sparks. It was all I wanted. It was all I could think about. My body had been ripe in so many ways, ready to be a full-course dinner for a vampire who happened to look like a Swedish supermodel. Lysander had taken the high road, and I'll probably never know why, but what I did know, suddenly and with certainty, was that the Silvano Clan had engineered this drug and were getting the Hammerskins to enforce distribution so that the vampires would have access to more willing humans.

Not just for an easy blood supply, to feed their fiendish appetites, but for a more sinister reason. The clan was growing their army.

I REMEMBERED the security footage video that Morgan had shown me in her office. The man walking in an odd manner, clearly feeling strange, and then a shadow swooping. A vampire had nabbed him, attacked him, and he had enjoyed it, because that was the essence of the drug. When the cops had asked him later that night what had happened, he said he couldn't remember, yet he was wearing a scarf around his neck. I'd bet my bottom dollar—and I didn't have a lot of those —that Dempsey was now a vamp initiate. Instead of draining him and discarding his body, they'd keep him on the addictive stuff till he was a full-fledged vampire, and then he'd be ready to join the Silvano army to prepare for the *coup* that everyone knew was coming. The Hammerskins wanted to rule the Realm, too, so between the two clans they must have struck some kind of deal. The vampires would raise the army, and the Hammerskins would make sure they had plenty of recruits.

I knew instantly that no matter how bad I felt, I needed to stop the Vampire Venom operation that night. Brutal withdrawal be damned. Burning shame be damned. I needed to shut that Venom lab down immediately, before they could trap any more untouched humans, before they could grow their vampire horde any more.

THE OTHER IDEA that came to me sitting there on the grimy kitchen floor was the realization that I didn't need to take the potion to *Mason & Sons* for a total lab analysis in a fancy spinning machine. We were out of Venom and out of time. Luckily for me, I had an even better idea. I picked up the lid again and carefully unscrewed the glass shard that was still attached to it. A small black coin remained. A magical credit. The token that was going to get us into the drug manufacturing lab.

"Gizmo?" I called.

I heard a thump on the bedroom floor, then the snow-colored ferret came scampering to me and landed on my lap. He seemed amused that I was sitting on the floor. I showed him the lid, and he took it from me, sniffing it and turning it in his paws as if it were a miniature steering wheel. For a moment I was anxious that he'd stick his tongue out and try to taste the potion residue, but I needn't have worried. Turns out that magical albino ferrets are a lot more clever than *girl wizards*.

"Do you think you can find it?" I asked him.

Gizmo nodded and looked at me expectantly, nose and whiskers at the ready.

I hauled my exhausted body off the floor, fetched my trench coat and crossbow, and I clipped my wand to my utility belt.

If I can shut down the lab, I thought, *maybe it will go a small way in making up for what had happened here with Lysander.*

I'd never be able to fully forgive myself, but it would be a damn good start.

CHAPTER 28

RIBBON OF SMOKE

I knew the Hammerskins would be watching the building, even though it was past midnight, so I pulled my collar up to obscure my face and sneaked out the back. The orcs would recognize my bike instantly if I were to roar out of there, so I was forced to walk. There were hardly any people walking the streets, and it felt eerie and deserted as I made my way north. Shop signs flickered as I walked past them, and the air smelled of trash and stale exhaust fumes. Gizmo directed me with his snout, like a furry compass needle, and after ten minutes of walking I felt my head clear.

I was going to shut down the lab, then go looking for Crowe. Easier said than done, seeing as she wasn't answering her phone.

Gizmo squeaked, and I stopped. He was looking at a nondescript door in the wall, one I wouldn't even have seen despite walking right past it. I tried the metal handle, and it was locked. I unclipped my wand.

"Ignem Exquiris," I said, and a current shot down my arm and out of the silver wand, melting the lock.

It felt good to have the wand back, even if I couldn't look at it without thinking of Lysander and feeling the acidic guilt boil inside me. I waited for the glowing metal to cool, looked behind me, then wrenched the door open and stepped inside.

THE DOOR SWUNG CLOSED behind me and I was left standing in a black box. I waited, wondering what would happen next. The enclosed space smelled of damp bricks.

"I think you took a wrong turn somewhere, Gizmo," I said, but then the floor I was standing on gave way and we dropped so fast it took my breath away, falling through a vertical portal with edges that shimmered with mercury. I held onto Gizmo, making sure I didn't lose him as we plummeted down, hoping for an easy landing for my aching bones.

I did not get my wish.

We slammed into the ground, and I got a mouthful of evil-tasting dust and a head full of stars. It took me a couple of moments to recover. When I opened my eyes, I saw that beyond the pile of old cardboard boxes which camouflaged us there was some kind of warehouse. A re-purposed shipping container the color of a rusted sunset. I couldn't make out where we were, but I guessed at someplace in the Orc SubRealm. The fetid stink that steamed off orcs was a dead giveaway.

My vision cleared, and I jumped up off the ground. The warehouse seemed to be deserted, apart from a pair of heavily armed grim-lipped guards that looped around and around the premises. I waited for them to pass me and turn the corner, then I scuttled toward the container and the makeshift entry that had been laser-cut into the side.

The lab was dark and quiet inside, and I didn't want to risk illuminating it with my wand. But I also didn't want to risk bumping into anything, or send something crashing to the floor. Soon my eyes adjusted to the low light and I moved as stealthily as I could manage, my boots making only the softest squeaking sound as I went.

I had expected a seedy kind of meth lab, but the interior of the compact factory was neat and clean and modded out with cutting edge tech. Ferra would have been impressed. Gallons of ingredients waited patiently in their shiny metal vats, and machines with blinking lights whirred quietly in the background.

Further into the minimalistic lab, the glass refrigerators that lined the walls were fully stocked with thousands upon thousands of vials of the sparkling cerulean potion, and the doors were locked not only with elaborate combination locks but also individual enchantment spells. This lab may be situated in the SubRealm and guarded by orcs, but this was no orc operation. I could tell by the attention to detail, the minimalism, the neatness. The vampires were the drivers here; the orcs were merely their henchmen.

I NEEDED a way to destroy the lab without getting nabbed by the beefy orcs in uniform. A stick of dynamite would have come in handy, or a magical grenade, but I had neither.

A memory floated in my mind; one I hadn't thought of in years. Sitting in the dimly lit lounge in my family home, at Dad's feet, while he and Mom watched a TV show called *MacGyver*. I was too young to follow the story, but Mom said something like, "*Now he'll make a bomb from some mouthwash and a shoelace,*" and I remember thinking that was funny. Dad smiled, too.

Well, it looked like I had no choice but to pull a MacGyver. I tried to remember the list of chemicals we were warned about in our potions class at the Copperfield Institute. The ones that were listed as highly unstable, flammable, oxidizing, corrosive, water-reactive. The ones we were warned to never, under any circumstances, mix together. I crouched down and started looking at the labels of the various lab supplies, drawn to the ones that were in heavy, protective containers with hazard labels stuck onto them. There was a row of especially enthusiastically stickered drums on the bottom row at the back, and I hauled them out. *Sodium*, said the one. *Hydrogen Peroxide.*

Bingo, I thought.

I worked as quickly and quietly as I could, grabbing an empty wooden barrel I had noticed at the front of the lab and rolling it toward the section of the makeshift building that held all the ingredients and the glass fridges stocked to capacity with the finished product. I placed the wide barrel in the middle of the floor and tipped in all the hydrogen peroxide I could find. It had a strong odor, and I hoped that the orcs outside wouldn't be able to smell it over their own diaper breath. I packed as much fuel as I could around the barrel: bags of sawdust, office paper, wooden chairs, anything I could find that would burn easily. I didn't want a flash in the pan. I wanted an explosion followed by a hungry fire. I wanted this whole place up in smoke and ash before anyone had the temerity to save it.

I emptied one of the bags of sawdust over the floor and then poured the sodium into the empty bag and knotted it tightly. Then I climbed up onto a stainless-steel trolley and strung the bag of sodium up from one of the lab lights above, with an edge pointing directly down into the barrel of H2O2. The bag was heavy, and it was tricky to tie it securely enough, especially with shaking fingers, in the dark. One false move and I'd be leaving the SubRealm in a Jax-scented ribbon of smoke.

Once, just as I almost lost my grip on the bag and accidentally incinerated myself, the beam of a flashlight cut through the dark, right in front of me. I froze, certain that I had been found out, spotted through the high narrow window. My heart was in my throat. But then the light disappeared and I could breathe again. Finally, I was able to string the bag up in the optimal position, and I was ready to get out of there. I took one more look at the vast quantity of Vampire Venom, each tiny vial representing a possible addition to the Silvano Clan army. The drug was also a reminder of what I'd almost done with Lysander, and how broken it had made me feel inside, as if I was a hollowed-out version of my real self. Maybe the destruction I was about to wreak would go some way toward recreating my true self, even if it was a damaged version.

I waited for the orc guards to circle around, then I crept out of the shipping container and back to my mountain of litter and boxes. Safely in the shadows, I watched them loop around a couple more times while I built up my courage. Despite my bravado in setting up the chemical bomb, I had never done anything like that before and I was nervous that it would work, and doubly nervous that it wouldn't. I guessed there was only one way to find out.

I was breathing fast when I unclipped the wand from my utility belt. If I thought the Hammerskins and the Silvanos were after me before, this stunt of mine would slingshot me to the very top of their respective hit lists. But there was no going back. No way would I allow the Venom to facilitate Acheron Baldassare's rise to power. Deep down, I knew I didn't really stand a chance of taking down the ambitious Silvano Clan, or the brutish Neo-Nazis, but I sure as hell was going to make it as difficult for them as possible.

Wand in hand, I waited for the next time the guards walked past me, and as soon as they were within spell-slinging distance I gathered my hatred for them and let it steam inside my chest. I felt my power glowing inside my body, and I concentrated it into a rush of magic eager to flow out of my hands.

One of the orcs stopped right in front of the pile of boxes, making me lose concentration, and my magic began to dissipate.

"Did you hear that?" he asked the other one.

Hear what? I thought. I hadn't moved a muscle.

The other orc grunted and shook his head. The first orc looked directly into the pile of boxes, and I held my breath. He didn't see me. Gizmo moved around in my pocket and I prayed to the Void that he didn't squeak or snuffle. I thought the guard would move away, but he frowned and lifted his automatic weapon, flicking off the safety, while the other one started nudging boxes and pieces of trash with the toe of his factory boot.

Fear replaced the hatred, and I began to whip up the power inside my core again, ready to counter-attack if the brutes found me. My original plan had been to spare these two guards' lives, but now it seemed they were intent on sniffing out death, and I would be ready for them.

CHAPTER 29

FIZZ AND CRACKLE

The orc security guards, bristling with weapons black and oily against their dark uniforms, got closer and closer to me. I considered an invisibility spell, but I thought it would be best to preserve as much magic as possible in case I'd need it to fight. A noisy elemental spell would be too dangerous; the men were too heavily armed. I knew from previous experience—my latest city brawl—that a distraction spell didn't work particularly well on orcs. And then I realized I didn't need a distraction spell. I had a real distraction all set up, in the form of a chemical bomb big enough to blow a hole in even the most ambitious vampire's plans.

I could smell the orcs as they got closer to me, and closer. Blue cheese and rotten tomatoes. Fishing bait. Yeast. I swallowed the bile that was rising in my throat. It would not have been a good time to retch. The shorter orc began kicking boxes out of the way, and punching the piles of trash. He was getting way too close for comfort. The other didn't let go of his AK47; I could see his itchy trigger finger tapping a tune.

I inhaled deeply, silently, even though the air tasted like orc, to calm my nerves and focus my power. It didn't help that they were right there, on top of me, and that I was still feeling tender from the Venom withdrawal.

Slinging a remote spell requires a great deal of concentration, but I was intent on making it work, and making it work quickly. I had perhaps thirty seconds to ignite my bomb and finish what I had gone there to do. I belted my bomb-proof coat closely around me and gathered the anxiety in my chest, the disgust and the fear, and started to fashion the power into a flame I could use. The tricky part was that I didn't want the flame on the end of my wand, but a hundred meters away, inside the lab, on the corner of that bag pointing down into the barrel. I had to imagine it exactly in order for it to work, but with the orcs rooting around right next to me it was extremely difficult to picture it perfectly. I closed my eyes, despite it making me more vulnerable, and I thought of the sack cloth bag. Thought of its dry hessian fibers. All I would need is to make a small hole, and the force of gravity would do the rest.

Ignem exquiris, I thought.

In my mind's eye I saw the flame licking at the bottom of the bag. I couldn't tell if it was my imagination or the spell really working, but soon the fibers in my imagination caught alight, and slowly the fire opened the bag by one squared millimeter, then four. At first the granules fell inconsistently and just made the solution below fizz and crackle, but soon the flow of the dry chemical gained momentum and ripped the bag open, and all the contents streamed downward. I expected a giant explosion to rip through the shipping container and slam us to the ground, but there was just the quiet of nighttime and the rooting of the guards. I heard one of them right next to me, and my eyes shot open at the same time as his automatic weapon clicked against my temple.

I swore under my breath.

The guard looked amused. "What we have here?" he said.

"What?" said the other one, and scratched his crotch.

"Girl," said the shorter one.

The scratcher came into view. "Restricted area," he said.

"Sorry," I said. "I was looking for the Beer Hall."

The muzzle of the gun pressed harder.

Why hadn't the bomb worked? Had I done something wrong? Mis-remembered the chemical reaction?

I cast my eyes over to the makeshift lab, but it remained still and quiet.

"I took a wrong turn," I said, smacking my forehead dramatically. "I've never been good at Portal Magic." At least that last part was true.

They looked at me, then at each other. "What must we do with her?"

"You don't have to do anything," I said. "I'll disappear."

"The only way you're going to disappear," said the taller one, "is if we make you disappear."

I could smell the cold metal, the gunpowder, and their barbecue sauce B.O.

I looked at the silent shipping container again. My spell hadn't worked. I had to retry, but for that I needed time, and these orcs weren't going to give me that luxury. The taller one grabbed me, wrenching my arm toward him, and pulled me out of my hiding place. My mind was whirring with the spells I could possibly use on them. I thought of the Hammerskin on the street that I had frozen, but before I could articulate the spell there was something disgusting wrapped over my head and in my mouth, a stinky gag, and the taller orc instructed the other one.

"Tie her up," he said. "Put her in the back of the lab. We'll deal with her once our shift is over."

"No!" I tried to say, but the gag didn't allow the word to escape my mouth. "No!" I shouted, shaking my head, struggling against the orc's meaty forearms and frankfurter fingers. My strength was a joke to him. He picked me up in one hand and began walking in the direction of the lab. In my mind I saw the flame again, eating into the hessian bag, allowing some of the sand-like chemical to drop into the volatile liquid below.

"No!" I kept shouting, and struggling against him, even though I knew it was pointless. "It's going to blow up!" I shouted, but the gag disguised my words. He carried my squirming body to the back end of the container, where there was a small, basic office and toilet, and he dumped me onto the floor, tying my limbs to my side tightly with thick rope.

"Wait!" I shouted. "Please!" but he just grunted at me and slammed and locked the door, leaving me writhing in the dark on the hard metal floor. That's when I finally heard the fizz and crackle of the chemicals next door.

CHAPTER 30

GLOWING METAL CARCASS

I struggled against the heavy rope, and against my gag. Luckily, after my nightmarish experience with the evil wizard, Slyden Abarim, I was well versed in escaping when tied up. My only worry was being able to do it fast enough to avoid being blown to Halloween Heaven. Abarim's ligatures had been made of enchanted black ribbon, which had been relatively easy to cut, but this rope was industrial strength, like something you'd find on a ship. The popping and snapping of the beginning of the chemical reaction was getting louder, and I knew it would be just moments before the whole container was incinerated like kindling at a Guy Fawkes celebration. Cutting through the rope would take too long, so I needed another strategy. I looked around the dark room, but nothing came to me. I could practically hear the clock ticking in my head. Ten seconds to my own personal Armageddon. At least the Vampire Venom would be destroyed, which would slow down the Silvano Clan's march to power. At least I would have redeemed myself in that small way.

Then I heard Gizmo squeak. I had forgotten he was sleeping in my pocket. It was one thing, sacrificing myself for the cause, but I didn't want to be responsible for my favorite ferret's demise. I'd have to use the *Rumpis* spell. I was avoiding using it because, firstly, I reckoned it was ill-advised to engineer an explosion just a couple of meters away from a vast amount of incendiary material. Also, because using a destruction spell on a binding against your body was a bad idea. The chances of it just destroying the thing you aim it at and not doing any damage to your own body is pretty slim. There have been stories of wizards who have tried to destroy their shackles or handcuffs but ended up destroying their hands, too. I was rather fond of my hands and I wanted to keep them. But the crackling was getting louder, and I guess that losing a hand or two was probably a better scenario than being instantly ashed like an out-of-luck vampire.

I took a breath and tried to ignore the tick-tock-tick-tock in my head. I focused on my fear, which felt like it was splattered all over my body. I swept it all together into a concentrated stream of power, and then as quickly and carefully as I could, I directed the magic toward the knot in the rope.

Rumpis! I thought, and there was a flash of white hot pain behind my back, and a crunching of cartilage which made me cry out, even though I was trying to be quiet. The rope smoked and fell to the floor. My trench coat had protected my back from the spell, but my exposed wrists were in agony, as if someone had hobbled my hands with a flaming sledgehammer. I didn't have time to inspect the damage; I was free of the restraints and I could smell the chemicals beginning to burn next door. I wrenched off the gag and stumbled to get outside. I tried the handle of the locked door, which sent a current of pain up my arm. My hands were limp and unable to reach for my wand, unable to blast the lock. I cried out in panic and frustration, wanting to slam my fists against the stubborn door. I was close to losing control then—the anxiety had vaporized my rational thinking. I wanted to scream and kick at the obstacle, and let loose a giant *Rumpis* spell that would blow up the entire SubRealm. Instead I swallowed my anger and leaned my forehead against the cool metal of the door.

Five seconds left? Three?

I was so used to being able to blast open the lock on any door, I felt completely trapped without being able to do it. Just thinking about it made my wrecked wrists flare with pain.

"Nano, key," I said, and my nano snaked out of my top pocket and folded inwards into a skeleton key. With hands glowing with agony I eased the key in and turned it, and the door opened.

"Nano, helmet," I said, and the key transformed into a

helmet. I stumbled down a stair I didn't remember, almost falling to the ground, then made a break for it.

"Hey!" said one of the guards. "Hey!" It was the trigger-happy one. I assume I had just made his day by breaking for it. His mate joined the party and I could practically hear the bullets being engaged in their shiny black automatic rifles.

I ignored their calls, sprinting as fast as I could to put as much distance as possible between my body and the ticking time bomb. They both began shooting at me at the same time, and the missiles zinged all around me, past me, and ricocheted off my helmet and bullet-proof trench coat with small golden sparks. They were gaining on me, and I could smell gunpowder and smoke and orc sweat, but none of it mattered, because then there was the mother of all explosions, a gigantic boom that would have burst my injured eardrum if it hadn't already been punctured by the Hammerskin the day before. There was a shock of white light and it echoed in my vision, stealing my sight. Even though the nano helmet muffled my hearing, I had never experienced anything so loud; the noise vibrated through my whole body and boiled my blood. The force of the explosion lifted me up off the ground. I cycled through thin air, the heat slamming against my back and whipping my body forward one final meter before crashing me down to the hard clay ground. The helmet smashed as I landed and sent streaks of light to my already shock-blinded eyes. I blinked them away and levered myself up onto my elbows, trying to see what had become of the lab. I could only make out vague shapes, but nonetheless was able to see that my mission had been accomplished. Just a glowing metal carcass remained, like long-dead whalebones, and it was burning in earnest, sending off eruptions of sparks like firecrackers.

Floating fire landed all around me, on top of me. A cinder, like a dragonfly made of flame, landed on one of my injured hands, and died. Debris fell to the ground as if we were in the aftermath of a tornado, including an unidentified piece of lab equipment, the shattered door of a glass fridge, and the singed forearm of a trigger-happy orc. I found I had no sympathy for him or his dance partner. The blast of the explosion had stripped my heart of emotions. I didn't have any feelings apart from cold relief that Gizmo and I were alive, and as he led me back to the portal, I stroked his head and told him that everything was going to be okay.

CHAPTER 31
THE MAGE AND THE WIZARD

When I got back to my apartment, I was ready to fall into the goblin-sized shower and then into bed, fantasizing about saying thank you to Ghost for the freshly laundered pajamas and then having seemingly infinite uninterrupted hours of dreamless sleep cuddled into Darick's strong body, waking up refreshed and ready to solve every last case on my to-do list. All of that was, however, to remain a fantasy, because as I traipsed past a drooling Gnor and opened my front door, I saw that I had company. Despite it being almost four o'clock in the morning, two people and a raven sat at my kitchen table, awkwardly drinking tea.

"Darick!" I shouted, and launched into his arms as he stood up, knocking over his tea and almost breaking the spindly chair in the process.

"Kresnik!" I said to the raven, so relieved that Bron was back. Darick hugged me like I'd never been hugged before, and we stayed like that for a full minute, feeling each other's warm skin, smelling each other, until we were satisfied that the moment was real.

"Jax," he murmured into my hair, which I was sure was scented with the Venom drug lab explosion.

"You're healed," I said.

As if he could sense the pain in my wrists, he lifted them up and inspected them, and I felt the tendons repair and cartilage mend. Then he put his hand over my injured ear and jaw, as if he was going to kiss me, and I felt the pain disappear, which was a good second prize.

"Thank you," I said, staring into his eyes; his perfectly unscarred face. He returned my gaze and we stood like that for a moment, locked into each other. I wished the rest of the world would disappear and it would just be Darick and me. The mage and the wizard.

A cat meowed, breaking our trance, and I looked down at the floor, puzzled. The raven gave the cat a beady eye.

"What's Celestine doing here?" I asked. She had her black coat on, with fizzing gold stars. She glared at me and meowed again, with urgency. That's when I remembered the other person in the room. Darick and I needed some serious catching-up time. He had something to tell me and I needed to know what had happened to him before he fell into his hibernation. But there was someone else at the table, and her news couldn't wait.

"Izzy's missing," said Paige. "I didn't know where else to go. She said you were helping us."

"*Faex,*" I swore. "I knew something was wrong. She agreed to come straight here after the cops finished questioning her at the fair."

"That was ten hours ago," said Paige, her eyes brimming with tears. "She told me she had one stop to make before coming here, but then her phone died. I assumed she was at the hospital, visiting Hettie, but they said she's not there. She's not at home, either."

"Where did she go?" I asked.

"I don't know!"

"She didn't give any kind of hint? Anything?"

Paige shook her head. "No."

Celestine meowed and scratched the charity-shop chair, which made Bron flutter his wings.

"But what did she say? What were her exact words?"

"I don't remember!" said Paige. "Hazel's body was being loaded up into the vehicle and we were all so distraught. The police kept asking us the same questions again and again. They were suspicious of Izzy because she wasn't with us in the forest when it happened."

"When what happened?" asked Darick.

"When the magic knocked us out, in the forest. She was the only one who wasn't with us. The lead detective really gave her a hard time."

I jumped to Morgan's defense. "Yes, well," I said. "She's a thorough investigator."

"It wasn't a woman," said Paige. "It was this bolshy guy in a new-looking uniform. Kept flashing his shiny badge. I think he was trying to impress people."

It was the new Council-appointed detective on the Scorpion squad. The wizard they were grooming to take over Morgan's job.

Faex, *why can't anything ever be simple?*

"Kresnik," I said, making the bird jump. "You saw what happened in the forest. Tell us!"

But the bird just looked at me with its cheeky beak, then started pecking at one of the black toffee apples on the table.

"Bron," I said. "Stop playing around. Turn!"

Bron looked at me, but remained a bird.

"The witch hunter," said Paige. "I think whoever knocked us out with that magic in the forest put a spell on Bron."

"He had a bird's-eye view in the forest," I said. "Bron knows who the killer is."

I SPLASHED water on my face and checked my crossbow, wishing I had time for a cup of coffee.

"I'm sorry to leave you just as you've woken up," I said. "I'll be back soon."

"Where are you going?" asked Darick.

"I have a deal to keep. I need to find Isadora Crowe."

"I'm coming with you," he said.

"No way," I shook my head. "You've done enough for me. And I've only just gotten you back."

"In that case," Darick said. "It looks like we're about to have our first argument, because there's no way I'm letting you go after a witch hunter on your own."

"I won't be on my own. I'll have Bron."

Bron cawed from the kitchen table, then continued to peck at the candied apples.

"I need you here," I said. "In case Crowe shows up."

"I can do that," piped Paige. "I'll wait here for her."

I glared at Crowe's assistant.

"Or not," she said, and looked away, blushing.

"Darick is staying here," I said. My decision was final.

I didn't want Darick to put himself in danger for me again. He had already barely survived the attack at the volcano pocket realm and who knows where he had to go to find Gizmo. Let's just say that if he weren't a self-healing mage he'd probably be nothing but a fond memory. But not even a mage can come back from the dead, and I didn't want to lose him for good.

"I'd rather die," said Darick.

I turned to face him. His eyes were electric. "What?"

"I'd rather die protecting you than live without you."

CHAPTER 32

STRANGER THINGS

Well, I thought, *that escalated quickly.* I've never believed in love at first sight—in fact I had found Darick rather infuriating at the beginning of our relationship—but now I couldn't imagine life without him, either. I didn't know how to respond when he said he'd rather die protecting me than live without me. I felt the same way about him. I don't have a romantic bone in my body, plus I've never been good at putting my feelings into words, but I knew that I would do anything to keep us intact. I swallowed hard and returned his intense gaze.

"Fine," I said. "We'll compromise."

Paige would stay at my apartment and call us if Crowe showed up. Darick would go to the hospital where Hettie Frost was lying insentient and barely breathing, and see if he could heal her. If he could get her well enough to talk, we'd be able to find out who buried her alive at the Moonlit Chapel. Then we could meet wherever the killer happened to be and hopefully it wouldn't be too late to save Isadora Crowe's life.

It was a good plan, apart from the fact that Hettie Frost may never wake up, and I didn't know where to start looking for Izzy while Darick worked his special brand of mage magic. I guessed I would continue my original plan, which was to speak to each of the witches individually to see if I could get any information about what had happened in that forest, at *Gallanrock*. In my experience, sometimes a witness doesn't think they remember anything, but when you draw the story out of them slowly, digging all the while, small details emerge that they didn't even realize they knew. I didn't know which of the coven members to choose first, so I was about to go eeny-meeny-miny-moe, but Kresnik was so focused on attacking that poisonous toffee apple that it gave me an idea. I remembered that there had been a plate of apples in Fidelis Wolfmoon's house, too, next to the abandoned cup of tea.

"Paige," I said. "Who made those toffee apples?"

Paige's face was as pale as the moon. "What?"

"The toffee apples."

"Ophelia Knox," said Paige. "She's really good in the kitchen. Loves to bake. She's always bringing treats to the gatherings."

"I'll start with her," I said, and held out my forearm. Bron flew over to me and perched on it, ready to go. Paige texted me the Knox couple's address, I saved it on my phone, and waved goodbye to her as I left.

BECAUSE OF THE imminent Hammerskin threat, I had to leave the building surreptitiously, walking a block westward before summoning my motorbike with my ring. Once I had my bike under me and accelerating, and the sun began to rise, life seemed a little easier to bear.

A call came in through my smart helmet bluetooth. The caller ID said SCORPIONS.

"Morgan," I said. "I've got something for you."

"Ooh," she said. "Then we can play *quid pro quo*."

"Why? What do you know?"

"You go first," she said.

"Well. That drug? That crazy rainbow snowflake?"

"Yes?"

"You don't have to worry about it anymore."

"What the hell does that mean?" she said.

"I'll fill you in on the details later, but you can close that case, for now. Concentrate on the V-Cult killers instead. Save your job."

Her sigh was like a wisp of smoke down the line. "I think it's too late for that."

"What?" I said. "Why?"

"They've already given the new case—your witch friend's case—to the new detective in the squad. Musubarin."

"The wizard," I said. "What are they playing at?"

"They said they needed faster results, and—"

"And?"

"And I can't blame them. Two witches dead on that Star-Dust case, one in critical condition. Plus almost a dozen women killed by the cult. All in a week, all on my watch. And what do I have? Nothing."

I think I heard her kick something, but it could have just been the static on the line.

"It's only been a week," I said. "You don't find serial killers in a week."

"According to the Council, this new guy does. In fact, he's probably already found Liz Durison's killer and is celebrating by having a drink with the boys. Probably forgot to send me the memo because I'm just a hack detective."

"Rubbish," I said. "Besides, it's barely five a.m. He wouldn't be celebrating with the boys now unless it was at Starbucks over cappuccinos and donuts."

"Stranger things," said Morgan. "Stranger things have happened. P.S., you're not helping. All you've done is made me crave donuts."

"You said you have something for me?"

"Oh! The reason I phoned," she said.

"Yes."

"So, you know you asked me to look into any other witch-related homicides?"

"Yes."

"There was this case in Cape Town a couple of months ago. The White Tree coven."

"Listening."

"A whole coven was killed over a week or so, but no-one put it together because it was, like, a covert coven? A closeted coven? I don't know what the right terminology is. No one knew they were witches. So, no one knew the murders were related until they found—"

"Until they found the adder stones," I said.

Morgan was quiet for a moment. "Yes," she said. "The adder stones. Then the coven pin, and some other clues. It was never investigated fully, though, because they don't have a paranormal crime unit down there."

"But if they weren't openly practicing witches, then how did the witch hunter find them?"

"Your guess is as good as mine. Forage? The dark web?"

"How many witches died?" I asked.

"It says that ten bodies were found. Two witches missing, presumed dead. No suspects."

"Brutal."

"And it could have happened before, too, you know. Cape Town was the only team to actually link the witches, but it could have happened in other cities without anyone putting those pieces together."

"Okay," I said. "Thank you."

I FOLLOWED my phone's directions to get to the Knox couple's house and parked in their immaculate driveway. They didn't answer the doorbell. Cheerful daisies and purple irises lined the path to the back door, which was locked.

"I guess we'll have to go to the next witch on the list," I said. Erik Tenebris. But when I walked toward my bike, Kresnik cawed and clawed my shoulder. I didn't speak raven, but I guessed he wanted me to keep trying to find them.

Oh, hex, I thought, *please not more dead bodies.* I pictured them in the kitchen, dead on the floor, with Ophelia's salted caramel boiling down to tar on the stovetop. I'd had enough corpses for the week.

"Ignem Exquiris," I whispered, with my hand on the round silver doorknob. The lock softened and I was able to open the back door. I looked both ways and entered the Knox kitchen. There were baking ingredients strewn around the room, which didn't look right for what looked like an otherwise neat and tidy house, and I got a bad feeling.

"Hello?" I called.

I've just broken into your house and I'm worried about your kitchen cleanliness.

I remembered the Khargol kitchen on that fateful night I'd found Don Vito dead in his bed. The kitchen had been the first bad omen: burnt meatballs, Napoletana sauce bitter and black. The smell will always stay with me.

The Knox kitchen was different. Nothing burning, nothing black. But it was clear that Ophelia Knox had left in a hurry. With a mounting sense of dread, I began to pad through the house, searching their empty rooms as I struggled to put the pieces together.

Ophelia Knox makes toffee apples for the rest of the coven.

The Knox Stardust cloaks looked newer than the rest of the coven's.

Their house still looked new. Not scruffy and cozy, the way regular family homes are, but everything appeared new, from the fake timber floors to the modern kitchen counter-tops and shiny oven. Their framed wedding photo was dated a couple of months back, and the background was Table Mountain.

I understood, then, that the Knox couple were newly married and new to the neighborhood, and the StarDust Coven. Which means that Dylan Knox had lived somewhere before, possibly Cape Town. I moved toward the garage and flicked the lights on.

There was a small workshop to the side of the room, and I knew—before I even saw what was on the table—that it usually carried engraving equipment. Equipment which was probably stored away somewhere now, out of the view of nosy girl wizards. To prove my suspicion, I spotted a white adder stone on the floor and reached to pick it up and slip it into my pocket. It was yet to be engraved.

"Filius Canis," I said, and Kresnik cawed and flapped his wings. "The witch hunter is Dylan Knox."

SOMETHING about it felt so evil to me. The way he had insinuated himself into the coven to eat it up from the inside. I felt disgusted by him and the way he had tricked everyone into trusting him, even his new bride, and Crowe. I thought of him burying poor old Hettie Frost in the cold dark earth, and how terrifying that must have been for her.

So frightening that she ended up scraping away the tips of her fingers on the coffin lid. How he had manipulated his wife into coercing the coven into the forest yesterday for the *Hexenwald*, because it was her first time and she was really looking forward to it. And how he had killed Fidelis Wolfmoon in her own bath, and hanged Hazel Shackleton above *Gallanrock*, a site known for its sacred forest magic. I felt sick to my stomach, but worse than that, I felt my anxiety cut into me. Dylan had Crowe, I was sure of it, and he'd probably kill his wife, too, if she got in the way. Or even if she didn't get in the way.

If I was a witch hunter—which, in a way, I now was—where would I take my target? Or perhaps I wouldn't have to force her to go to any particular location. If I knew the potential victim, I would just arrange to meet her somewhere convenient.

I was getting somewhere, but before I could finish my thought process, my phone began to ring. The sudden sound was so loud in the dim garage that it made me jump, and casued my heart to pinball inside my chest.

"Hello?" I said, and my voice sounded odd and breathless.

"I'm at the hospital," said Darick. "Hettie Frost is talking."

"Oh, thank the Void," I said.

"I think I know where the killer is keeping Crowe."

I was about to answer when I heard a car's tires squeal to a halt outside the garage, and the double door began to lift, shuddering on its rails.

CHAPTER 33
SPARKS JUST BENEATH THE SKIN

I swore, slipping my phone into my pocket and searching for something to duck under, somewhere to hide. But a man ran under the half-opened door and tackled me as if we were in the final minutes of a World Cup rugby match. I scrambled away from him, crawling on the concrete floor, but he grabbed my ankle. When I looked back at him, ready to kick him in the face, I expected to see Dylan Knox, but someone else entirely was gripping my leg.

"Leave me alone!" I shouted, and followed through with the kick, and there was a loud crunching sound as my boot heel crashed into the bridge of his nose, crushing it. That's when I saw his badge glint, and noticed that he was in uniform. The man cried out in pain and grabbed his nose, letting go of my leg. I scrambled away from him and unclipped my wand. The other men jumped out of the Scorpion squad car and planted themselves on the driveway, reaching for their guns and wasting no time in aiming them at my—rather surprised—face.

"What the *faex*?" I said. "What is going on?"

The detective's uniform didn't look quite so new now, spattered with blood and dusted with gray. He kept one hand on his smashed nose and the other one out toward me, as if I were a wild animal, ready to pounce.

"Jacquelyn Denna Knight," he said. "You're under arrest."

I guffawed. "You're kidding. Right?"

Kresnik, who had flown outside during the scuffle, called, but only I seemed to hear him.

The man pinched his nose. "Not kidding."

"We're going to need you to get into the police vehicle, ma'am," said one of the officers.

"On what charge?" I asked.

"Breaking and entering," said the detective. I looked at his name badge, punctuated with the red Scorpion tail I knew so well.

DETECTIVE MUSUBARIN.

I remembered the name. Tilexon Musubarin. Sounded like old wizard blood to me. Morgan had told me about him being sent in by the Council to take over her position.

"Breaking and entering," I repeated after him. I couldn't deny that. In the last forty-eight hours I had broken into Fidelis's house, the Vampire Venom lab, and, where I stood, I was caught pretty much red-handed in the garage of the Knoxes.

"And conspiracy to commit murder," Tilexon said.

"Er, what now?"

The officers were watching my every move, ready to pump me full of lead if I tried to make a break for it. I didn't recognize any of their faces. They weren't Morgan's guys. The wizard must have brought his own team along with him.

"Your fingerprints were found in the deceased, Wolfmoon's, house."

"That's because I found her body," I said.

"After breaking into her house," he countered. "You were also at the scene of the attempted murder of Hettie Frost—"

"I can explain that," I said.

"—and in the forest when Shackleton was killed."

"If you put it that way..."

"We also have witnesses that say they saw you arguing with Isadora Crowe before finding Shackleton's body."

"Yes," I said.

"And now Crowe is missing, and you're standing here, breaking into another of the coven members' houses."

"Well," I said. "I can see how that may look bad."

Musubarin smirked. "How were you planning on killing the Knoxes, Ms. Knight?"

"I wasn't."

The detective gestured at one of his men. "Search her," he said.

The man tucked his weapon back into his holster and approached me. I put up my hands. In the outer right pocket of my trench he found the adder stone, which he showed to his boss.

"Ah," said Tilexon, inspecting it.

"I found it here," I said. "Near the engraving equipment."

He looked over my shoulder. "I don't see any engraving equipment."

I turned around. It was true. I knew that table was used for engraving, but all the wizard detective saw was a workshop table. I couldn't explain how I knew what it had been used for. Sometimes I could look into a glass and instinctively know which liquid had been in it before it had been washed and dried, but I couldn't tell Tilexon that. He'd lock me up for sure.

"Look," I said. "We can talk about the details later. But I know who the witch hunter is, I need to stop him."

"Get in the vehicle," said Musubarin.

"Crowe will die if I don't find her right now," I said.

"We can discuss it at the station."

I shook my head. "It'll be too late."

"Tell me who the killer is," he said. "We'll pick him up."

No way I was going to give him Dylan's name. The last thing I needed was him and his enthusiastic new team bumbling all over my case and getting people killed.

"Once Crowe is safe," I said. "I'll tell you everything I know."

Musubarin took a menacing step toward me. "What I don't think you understand," he said, "is that you're under arrest. We tell you what to do and how to do it, not the other way around."

"Why did the Council appoint you?" I asked. "You're not half the detective that Captain Morgan is."

He narrowed his eyes at me.

"If you even had a hint of Morgan's sniffer instinct, you wouldn't be here with me, wasting time while someone else's life is in danger."

"Get in the car," he snarled. The officer with the dark hair snicked off the safety catch on his revolver, and the sound made us all pay attention.

"I'm not going with you," I said. "Now you can make this easy, or you can make this difficult. Either way, I'm not hanging around."

I have an old enemy to save.

"One last chance, Knight," said the detective, reaching for his handcuffs.

I was not going to get tied up again.

Nope, no way. Not gonna happen.

The sight of the silver bracelets made something inside me snap. I was so sick of these bloody brutes thinking that I was just something to be tied up and gagged. Slyden Abarim, the security guard orcs at the Venom lab, and now the new detective on the block. My body was screaming NO. And with my heightened emotion came the tell-tale signs of my potential power. My fingers began to tingle and I could feel the magic inside, sparks just beneath the skin.

USUALLY I WOULDN'T RECOMMEND ATTACKING a police officer, especially not a shiny new Council-appointed detective who is trying to prove his worth. I certainly wouldn't recommend kicking said detective in the balls and making a run for it, but I happened to be in extraordinary circumstances. The Council was going to crucify me; they'd send me to the Boulderkeep labor camp for sure. But a girl wizard's got to do what a girl wizard's got to do, and in this case, I wasn't going to stand around kowtowing to an arrogant cop's whims while a psychopath had Izzy in his clutches.

No sir, no sirree.

So, with my best karate kick—okay, I'll be honest, it's my only karate kick—I whipped up my knee and gave him what-for with the heel of my boot he was coming to know so well. As my foot connected with his toolbox, I grabbed my wand and blasted a motion-freezing spell at the other officers.

"Impedio!" I yelled, and my magic flew out of my wand and smashed into them like a bowling ball of light. Tilexon was groaning and holding his crotch, and as he looked up at me, I raised my eyebrows at him and slung the same spell at him. He managed to hold up his palm.

"Effectus Adversum," he muttered, and the spell bounced off his hand, toward me. I dove to the side and it missed me by an inch. I had forgotten the man was a wizard. I recovered, and stared at the detective.

"I don't want to hurt you," I said, wand outstretched, walking backwards. "Let me go."

I moved out, into the orange light of the sunrise, and pointed my wand at the garage door mechanism.

"Fiat Fulgar!" I shouted, and a lightning bolt shot out of my wand, frying the circuitry in the command box. The heavy door slammed down, closing Musubarin inside. Bron the raven was waiting for me on the handlebar of my bike.

Five seconds later I was roaring off on my bike, with Bron flying overhead, hoping I'd never see Tilexon again, but somehow knowing that this was to be the beginning of a dangerous, difficult, and severely unfulfilling relationship. One that would most likely get me landed in one of the more terrifying magical prisons. But I couldn't afford to think about that, then. I focused on the road and twisted my handle to accelerate. I had a witch hunter to find.

CHAPTER 34

DEAD BLACK BRANCHES

"Dial Darick," I said to my smart helmet. He picked up on the first ring.

"Sorry about that," I said. "Someone tackled me while you were talking."

"What?" said Darick.

"I know. Some people can be so rude."

"Tell me where you are," he said.

"Not necessary. I got rid of them."

"I couldn't hear what was going on."

"Nothing," I said, remembering the look on Musubarin's face when I had kicked him. "No big deal."

Until they lock me up in a clammy cold basement for the rest of my life.

"I'm on my bike. Tell me where to go."

"Frost has been rambling, barely making sense," he said. "But she keeps mentioning a church. The Moonlit Chapel."

"Probably because that's where she was attacked, and buried."

"That's what I thought, too, but then she started to insist that Crowe is there, right now. And when I pushed her on it, she said something about knocking. I don't know, knocking on the coffin lid?"

"Knox," I said. "The witch hunter is Dylan Knox, but he's not at home."

"I think they're at the chapel," said Darick. "It makes sense. It's where it all began. Plus it has... cultural significance. I'll meet you there."

"What now? Cultural significance?"

"You know. The lore of the witches' crop circle."

"I have no idea what you're talking about. Speak to me as if I'm a toddler."

"The crop circle at the Moonlit Chapel is infamous," he said. "Centuries ago they rounded up a couple of Jo'burg witches and burned them there. Then back in the 40s or so, a huge pentagram was burnt into the ground, overnight, like a charred crop circle, except that nothing has ever grown back. Magical folk say it's the wrath of the dead witches, and anyone stupid or careless enough to enter the circle will be cursed for eternity."

I leaned into the curve of the road. "Just as I thought my day was looking up," I said.

I ARRIVED at Moonlit Chapel as the pink and orange sunrise turned to gold. I moved as fast as I could but tried to keep my nerve. I didn't want to go sprinting in there, tripping on a tree root, blowing my cover and getting Crowe killed. I looked up at the chapel, and despite the morning light, it seemed larger and more menacing than before. Now that I knew its history, I was more hesitant to enter. Off the ramshackle roof cascaded a sense of evil that I could feel swirling around me and turning my skin to braille. A part of me wanted to wait for Darick to arrive, but I knew that Crowe may not survive that long.

I crept up the path to the abandoned building, bruising the pine needles with my boots, trying to keep the sound of the crackling dead leaves to a minimum. I held onto the trunks of the trees that I passed, sometimes for support, sometimes because I needed to feel their bark to keep calm and grounded. Bron flew ahead of me and I found myself wishing I was good at shifter magic. I would have loved to have flown along with him, and getting a bird's-eye view of the crop circle would have been helpful, indeed.

When I reached the chapel, it was deserted and smelled of urine and dead candlesticks.

Eau de Haunted Chapel.

I took a deep breath despite the smell, and kept going, using the side door that Clementine had shown us at the gathering. As I stepped through the doorway, a strange thing happened. It was instantly night time, and cold. I blinked, trying to get used to the sudden blanket of darkness. I tried to step back into the chapel, just to work it out, but a pane of smoked glass now sealed the door, keeping me on the side of midnight. It was some kind of temporary portal, I realized. Someone didn't mind my arrival, but they weren't going to let me go. I stood with my hand on the strange, magical glass, looking inside at the day-time chapel, but the outside was painted the color of night.

Breathe, I told myself. *Breathe.*

I was pretty sure that Darick wouldn't be allowed access, and Bron would see that the crop circle was empty and fly back to me. But I wouldn't be in that daytime dimension anymore, so he wouldn't be able to find me. I was all on my own.

Alone, looking for a psychopathic witch hunter who knew I was approaching, in the dark haunted chapel grounds. Sometimes I really wondered about my sanity. No one was forcing me to do this job. I could give it up at any time and do something less dangerous. I could wake up in the morning and go in to the office. Chat to my open-plan neighbor. Swap chicken pilaf recipes. Sharpen pencils. Get to bed at a reasonable hour. Wear pencil skirts. I could, but I knew I wouldn't, not while evil like this existed.

There was a scuffling sound in the darkness, and I whipped around. I thought I caught a glimpse of a cape, but I wasn't sure.

Oh, great, I thought. As if that midnight portal wasn't complicated enough. There were vampires here. Of course there were. An evil portal like this would be an instant vamp-magnet. My nerves started to flicker, my pulse flared. The mist started to roll in, as mist tends to do around haunted chapels, but this time it was different. It was a sinister black fog scented with death and depravity, and I almost choked as it reached into my mouth and nostrils. I walked toward the cursed crop circle. The wildflowers and grass that grew where the pentagram was not charred was high, taller than I was, and it turned the crop circle into a black maze. I heard someone cry out from within—it was Izzy—and I automatically reached for my crossbow. I stepped into the narrow corridor and began navigating it, turning left and right and left again, doing my best to follow the sound of her voice.

As I WADED DEEPER toward the middle of the pentagram-shaped maze, I began to hallucinate. While that may sound like fun, I assure you it was not. Not while my heart was already trying to escape my ribcage and my limbs were numb with fear. The worst thing about the hallucinations was that they weren't in the distance, easy to put out of one's mind. They were right there, right in front of my eyes, jumping out at me. It was the figments of the witches' wrath I could see, and I felt their sense of confusion, disbelief, indignation and fury. I watched as the villagers jostled me with their sharp elbows and pitchforks, and felt their panic up close against my skin. There were smoking torches all around me, and people in rags barreling through the maze and baying for the wicked women to be put to death. It was like I had time-traveled to the 1800s, in Salem, but this time I had a feeling the magical folk were going to be the ones who had the last laugh. I allowed the peasants to sweep me along with them, surfing the mob into the center of the maze, and as soon as I got to the central clearing, the hallucinations disappeared, and I stood, hardly breathing, looking at the huge bonfire laid out in the middle. Isadora Crowe saw me and screamed through her gag, a dirty red cloth that was tied tightly around her mouth. She was still wearing her medieval gown, trussed up against a tall log that was the centerpiece of the bonfire. Below her lay old chapel timber chairs, smashed into kindling and covered with dead black branches.

She screamed into her gag again, and I dropped my crossbow and ran to untie her. Crowe looked terrified, and she screamed even louder. When I realized she was trying to warn me, it was too late. I felt something smack me on the back of my head, and I went tumbling face-first to the scorched ground, below Izzy's desperately kicking feet, and my vision faded to black.

CHAPTER 35
ELEGANT POISONER

The smell of the smoke and the heat of the fire burning below me roused me from my unconscious state. At first, I wasn't sure what was going on, but then I remembered the night portal, the pitchforks, and the huge pile of dry kindling; the thunk as something large and heavy cracked against my skull. My head was pounding. I looked down and saw the flames below starting to lick my boots and could hear Crowe struggling behind me. We were tied to the old log back to back.

Latin swear-words exploded in my head; every curse and dirty word I knew. This is not how I wanted to die. Tendrils of white smoke reached up and caressed me as the fire crackled below, already gaining momentum as it leapt from twig to twig.

"Calm down!" I shouted at Crowe, and her body movements slowed. "It's no use flailing."

She may have thought I meant, *don't fight the Grim Reaper, when it's time, it's time,* but that's not what I meant at all. We needed some seriously creative spell-casting right then, and that wasn't going to happen if she was panicking.

I didn't have my crossbow, and I couldn't reach my wand, but I was scared enough to sling some potent magic. My body was thrumming with it.

But then Dylan Knox stepped into view, and Crowe started struggling again. I could smell her expensive maroon brocade dress burning and it made me feel sick. I knew that the smell of cooking flesh would come next.

"Please," I said to Dylan. "Don't do this."

My own feet started burning, and I couldn't help but kick, too. My plea didn't register on his face. He looked like a robot, an automaton. As if he were a puppet following someone else's commands. He threw more dead wood onto the fire.

"Stop it with the kindling," said a female voice. "I want them to burn slowly."

Ophelia Knox stepped out of the shadows. She was wearing a long white lace dress and she virtually glowed in the moonlight.

Despite the heat rising up from below, I felt like someone had splashed ice water in my face.

Izzy started to cry. I imagined the pebble in her pocket: the adder stone engraved with the elemental symbol for fire. A death threat writ in stone.

"I want to see them squirm," the wicked woman said. Her eyes were wet black marbles, the same inky spheres that I'd seen before.

The dominoes in my head started falling. I had been so dense. Why hadn't I worked it out, that Ophelia was the witch hunter? Apart from the red herring that was Shackleton's criminal record, all clues pointed to Ophelia. She was new to the city and new to the coven. She wore the shade of lipstick that was on the abandoned tea cup in Fidelis Wolfmoon's house. She was the one who hustled the coven into the forest while Crowe and I were arguing. And for the first time it occurred to me that she was an elegant and efficient poisoner.

I had thought the witch hunter must be a man, or at least an athletic woman, but Ophelia was neither. The only way she would have been able to drown Wolfmoon was to drug her, first. She had brought the toffee apples to Wolfmoon's house, perhaps slipped something into her tea. I remembered the flour scattered on the marble counter at her house, earlier, and she had dished up the scones at the medieval fair yesterday. Every one of the witches ended up blacking out at *Gallanrock*, giving Ophelia enough time to string Hazel up from that gazebo, with the help of her new husband, Dylan, who was certainly under the influence of some kind of potion. Bron had eaten a scone, too, and now he was stuck in his raven form.

OPHELIA KNOX HAD KILLED the members of the White Tree coven in Cape Town. She had killed every one of them except the strong male witch in the group, who she had managed to seduce into marrying her.

Ten bodies were found, Morgan had said. *Two witches missing.*

They couldn't stay in Cape Town. There would be too many questions asked. So, they had moved to Jo'burg and found the StarDust Coven. I started coughing. The acrid smoke filled my lungs and stung my eyes. I tried to rise above the pain and stay focused. No one was coming to rescue me. I had to get us out of this.

"How many covens have you destroyed?" I asked Ophelia, over the crackle of the fire. "How many times did you insinuate yourself into a group of witches, only to pick them off, one by one, in your sick hunting game?"

She laughed, and I heard real mirth in the sound, and surmised that she was a true psychopath. Even worse: she was a psychopath with delusions of grandeur.

"Why?" I asked her. "Why do you do it?"

"The scripture is very clear," said Ophelia. "Thou shalt not suffer a witch to live." I wished I could slap her.

Suddenly her smile turned to a snarl.

"I said leave the fire alone!" she shouted, and Dylan stopped in his tracks and dropped the dry sticks on the ground.

Ophelia rolled her eyes. I had a feeling that for her, having a new husband—even if you could magically pilot his every move—was more trouble than it was worth.

She turned her attention back to me, and began an incantation. It was in an ancient language, and I didn't understand the spell. The veins around Ophelia's inky eyes began to darken, and her face looked like it had been dusted with chalk and charcoal. The magic started taking control of her body, and it was as if she were talking in tongues. She spread her arms out as if welcoming the black of the night into her heart.

Usually I think of myself as pretty tough, but there was something so creepy about what she was doing that my terror made me look away. The flames were reaching higher.

Crowe began to scream again, and this time I didn't tell her to keep quiet. The fire was burning me, too, and my boots were melting. Crowe, who was barefoot, had it much worse. I closed my eyes and tried to still my raging brain. I knew I could still sling magic without my wand and the use of my hands. I just needed to cut everything else out and focus. Which is easier said than done, when you're busy being roasted like a rotisserie chicken at a Woolworths deli counter.

If I used a *Rumpis* spell on our binding, I'd be in danger of seriously injuring myself as I had done the night before at the Vampire Venom lab in the SubRealm. I couldn't risk that. Dealing with Ophelia was one thing, but I could sense there was more than just her evil to contend with in this midnight portal. It's like I could feel the shadows being drawn to us; black moths to a flame.

That gave me an idea. *How about fighting fire with fire?*

CHAPTER 36

A WITCH IN A WEDDING DRESS

There was movement on the perimeter of the maze. Ophelia and I both turned our heads at the same time, but she didn't look surprised. She had clearly been expecting company.

I—optimistically expecting Darick to arrive and sweep me off the pyre—was a little more than disappointed to note that it was neither Darick nor Bron, but instead a rage of skinhead orcs, baying for my blood. The Hammerskins were armed with pistols, automatic rifles, daggers and shivs, and had arrived to seek justice for what I had done to their street cred, and to their Venom lab. They spotted me immediately, lit up as I was, and stormed toward me.

"I used a special enchantment on the chapel door," Ophelia said. "I sent an open invitation to anyone in the dark side of the Realm who wished you evil."

"Of course you did," I said. "You don't like getting your hands dirty."

I was angry and scared, and my body was humming with new magic, and the entrance of the Hammerskins was my cue to use it.

Fire with fire, I thought.

"Ignem Exquiris!" I shouted, and all the emotion I had in my chest burned through my arms and shot down into the fire. My fire was more potent, and in a flash of flame the Hammerskins cried out and shielded their faces from the blaze. My blast blew the original bonfire into scattered piles all around us, barely big enough to toast a marshmallow. Crowe's body collapsed against her trusses.

"Get her!" commanded Ophelia, pointing her ivory wand at me, and for a second I thought the orcs might obey her, but then one of the more ogre-ish looking thugs scooped her up.

Silly witch, I thought, *inviting evil in, and thinking you can control it.*

She should have known that a Neo-Nazi orc wouldn't obey a witch in a wedding dress. Ophelia shrieked and thrashed against him, but he didn't even seem to notice, like King Kong batting off a couple of army helicopters and taking it in his stride. In the meantime I was loosening the singed knot in the rope that had us lashed to the tree. The burnt-brittle cord gave way and Crowe and I dropped unceremoniously to the ground.

Dylan Knox was ambling around the inner circle of the maze like a decapitated chicken. He reminded me of the train conductor at *Olde Worlde Railways* who hadn't yet realized he was dead. I don't even think he noticed the arrival of the orcs, despite their assault on his psychotic bride. One of the savages picked me up and was about to head-butt me when another orc stopped him.

"They want her alive," he grunted, and the orc who was holding me in the air let out a disappointed sigh. It's hardly an exaggeration to say that his breath made me wish I had died in the fire.

My crossbow was lying on the edge of the inner circle, in the dark, so no-one had noticed it yet. It was my only chance. I bit down on the orc's fingers—which was quite as disgusting as it sounds—and at the same time I kicked him hard in the stomach. He swore and let me go, shaking his bruised hand and checking for damage. While he was inspecting his frankfurters, I rushed toward my crossbow and scooped it off the ground, clicked the safety off, and took aim at the orc closest to me.

His face was the picture of fury when I pulled the trigger and the high-tech heat-seeking bolt speared him in the chest. He fell flat on his face right in front of me. I fired again, and again, picking off a dozen orcs with a dozen arrows. There were still three left, and when I pulled the trigger again, the crossbow just clicked impotently. The Hammerskins smiled and strode toward me, brandishing their glinting weapons. It was time for magic.

"Glaciem Exquiris!" I shouted and pulled the trigger at the same time. A javelin of ice flew out of my hand and through the crossbow, impaling the orc closest to me.

"Glaciem Exquiris! Glaciem Exquiris!" I shouted, and sent icicles through the other orcs' hearts, too. I was breathing heard, and turning from side to side, looking for more enemies, including Ophelia and the orc who had taken her. Crowe was still lying on the ground, her feet blackened and blistered by the beginnings of the bonfire. I thought of dragging her body out of the center of the maze, out of danger's way, but a new wave of orcs streamed through into the circle.

Faex, I thought. I was out of bolts, and my arm had taken a beating from the ice spells. My fingers felt brittle and numb from the cold, and not ready to dispense any more spells. I looked at the Hammerskin striding toward me, and realized with a flush of anxiety that I recognized his face. It was Zargulg, my old SubRealm flame, my Troll-lager-swilling crotch-singed one-nippled attacker.

Perfect, I thought. *Just perfect.*

Zargulg roared at me, and I was almost knocked out by his stench. He grabbed me—for a moment I was weightless—and he flung me to the ground, smashing my already bruised head on the earth.

"Fiat Ful—" I tried to send an electric current his way, but he slammed his meaty mitt over my mouth and I couldn't breathe or think.

Fiat Fulgar! I shouted in my head. *Fiat Fulgur!* But my fear had scattered my thoughts and, along with it, my energy. The spell wasn't taking. Zargulg let go of my mouth, and I took a huge gulp of air. Then he wrapped his massive hands around my neck and started throttling me. His hands were so strong the suffocation felt immediate. There was so much pressure on my throat that I thought I might instantly pass out. No air was going in; my lungs were screaming. Zargulg's slimy saliva streamed down on me, his face was swollen with effort. I tried to throw him off but he was the weight of a small- to medium-sized elephant. In a battle of bulk, he was the uncontested winner. I needed to find another way to beat him, but I couldn't breathe and I couldn't gather my energy. My focus was gone, my magic was a stagnant pool in my chest. The capillaries in my eyes burst and my brain began to shut down.

CHAPTER 37

THEY WANT HER ALIVE

My consciousness was fading to a blip when Crowe came into sight. She looked magnificent in her charred maroon dress as she loomed in the night sky, above Zargulg's murderous face, like a goddess, like the High Priestess that she was.

"Get thee to Hades!" she shouted at Zargulg, and tapped his shoulder. "Hades!"

He stopped strangling me, blinked once, then his body collapsed over mine. I gasped for oxygen, dragging the air into my lungs, staring at the sky while Isadora pulled his body off mine. I was dizzy and couldn't see straight, but when I sat up, I saw the ground littered with dead orcs.

"That was impressive," I choked out.

"It's the less cruel option of the two Death Spells I know," she said, tucking her red spellstick into her belt.

Who needs friends, I thought, *when you have enemies like Isadora Crowe?*

I was immediately envious of her witchcraft. She made magic look so easy. Wizard Death Spells were a whole lot more complicated, and a whole lot more dangerous, so we hardly ever used them. But then I realized that my envy of Isadora had never gotten me anywhere, and I was ready to forget our previous quarrels. I'd forgive her for everything, even the time she'd put superglue in my tooth-whitener paste. Crowe extended her hand and helped me up. My body was a jangling mess of nerves.

"Shall we get out of here?" she said. I picked up my crossbow and we walked together to the edge of the inner circle of the black pentagram maze, avoiding stepping on the bodies of the Hammerskins. Neither Dylan nor Ophelia were anywhere to be seen.

"Hold on," Izzy said, and walked back over to what was left of the bonfire. She felt in her pocket and pulled out the engraved adder stone, and tossed it into the fire. It caught alight, sending out orange sparks, and then burnt with dark purple flames.

WE HURRIED BACK to the chapel, and I should have felt light with the knowledge that we had escaped both the witch hunter and the orcs relatively unscathed, but something was bothering me. Ophelia was still on the loose, and I for one was not going to get a good night's sleep if she wasn't locked up where she belonged. Plus, I kept hearing that orc's voice. The one who'd said *they want her alive.*

As Isadora and I arrived at the chapel and stepped out of the night gateway and back into the daylight, there was a blur of a teal-lined cape and a vampire stood in my way. He smashed the crossbow out of my hand and it clattered to the floor. I quickly stashed my wand inside my coat. Crowe gasped and took a step backwards, into the arms of another vampire. Before she had time to utter her potent Death Spell, he gently touched her third eye and she lost consciousness.

I didn't recognize the face of the vampire that stood before me, but I could tell by his age and diamond-encrusted V-Cult brooch that he was a head honcho in the Silvano Clan. His hair was dark and greased back, *a la* Dracula, and he had mastered the art of the sneer.

"Filius Canis," I said. "I knew it. I knew one of you would be here."

"Wizard," he said. "I've heard a lot about you."

Part of me was too traumatized and too exhausted to deal with vampires, and I wanted to melt into the floor, and/or go home to bed and sleep forever. The other part of me, the part of me that despised the creatures with a white-hot passion, clutched my hidden wand and got ready to use it.

"Who are you?" I asked. "Deadwing's replacement?"

"Deadwing was a fool to let you get away," said the vampire, whose name came to me unspoken. *Demetrius.* A dozen more vampires swooped in, and landed behind him. They looked at me with cold, dead eyes. Demetrius took a step forward, and the others followed.

"We've been willing to look the other way, Jacquelyn Denna Knight," he said. "As a favor. As long as you behaved yourself."

"A favor to who?" I asked, but he ignored the question.

"It was a mistake." He didn't take his eyes off me, and cracked his knuckles. "Your destruction of the lab... has set us back considerably."

Ah, well, I thought to myself. *I may be dying tonight but at least I got something right.*

A female vampire hissed at me, showing her fangs. "Finish her!"

"Acheron wants her alive," said Demetrius, not without disgust.

"It's a mistake," said the female vampire, and hissed at me again. Demetrius turned to her and struck her hard with his palm, and she cried out in surprise, her hands flying up to hold her cheek.

"That will be the last time you question your king," he said, "or you'll be nothing but ash and bone. Do you understand me?"

She glared at him, and he took her silence as agreement.

"Besides," he said, leering at me. "You won't be disappointed when you see what Acheron has in store for this wizard."

This seemed to cheer the female vampire, and she smirked.

"Get her," she said, and the rest of the vampires flew toward me in a blur.

MY HEART WAS GOING CRAZY, my adrenaline flooded my body, priming it for magic, as I felt the vampires descend on me, grabbing at me, ready to take me away. My hand had recovered since my battle with the orcs. I gripped my wand and jabbed the vampire closest to me in the chest.

"Fiat Fulgar!" I yelled, and the wand electrocuted him and the other two vampires at his side. This made the other vamps go mental, and they forgot Demetrius's instructions and went for my throat.

"Nano. Collar!" I shouted, and my nano leapt out of my pocket and wrapped around my neck to protect it from their fangs.

They scowled at me and clutched me harder. Demetrius yelled at them to keep their cool. The female vampire had moved behind me, but I didn't notice till she had grabbed my wand.

She leaned in, putting her lips close to my ear. I could practically feel the sharpness of her fangs on my neck. "You're coming with us," she whispered.

CHAPTER 38

SHE WORE HER BRUISES LIKE A QUEEN

We stopped when we heard a bird's wingbeat. A black raven had flown into the chapel. It was Bron, and he had brought reinforcements. I had expected to see Darick—*where the hell was Darick?*—but in strode Lou in her post-apocalyptic hooded coat, holding an oriental sword across her body. She may be a city-street drug dealer, but in that chapel, in that moment, she strode in like a boss. Lou looked like Realm Royalty, her coat flaring out behind her, her quinine eye glowing like a neon light. She wore her bruises like a queen.

Confused, some of the vampires fell back, and some approached her. She took the audacious ones out first, jumping up into a roundhouse kick, bashing the first vamp unconscious and decapitating the other three in one elegant sweep of her djinn blade.

Then she landed neatly and brandished the red-stained sword again. "Who's next?"

It was completely surreal, and I had to blink and pinch myself to make sure I wasn't dead or dreaming. But I didn't stay frozen to the spot for long. I wrenched my wand back from the female vampire and immediately hurled a lightning spell her way.

"Fiat Fulgur!" I shouted, and hot lightning raced through my arm and bolted toward the vampire. She tried to dodge it, but it still got her on the shoulder and she hissed in pain. She turned back to me and showed me her fangs.

"Glacium Exquiris!" I said, and I funneled a giant shard of ice her way. It pierced her ribcage and staked her to the ground, where she screamed and thrashed about, and then combusted, leaving only yellow sparks and ash behind. The vampires were six down, but we still had six to take care of, including the honcho, who was coming my way.

The three vampires behind me didn't fancy their chances with Lou much and tried to retreat, so Lou had to go after them. They got to keep their heads, but received a convincing stab to their internal organs instead. One of them, not quite dead, reached out and grabbed Lou's ankle, forcing her to trip and fall, and he went for her neck. I was too far away to stop him from attacking her, and Demetrius was in my way. I cried out and tried to get to her, but he stopped me, so Crowe beat me to it. I hadn't seen her wake up, but for the second time that night she had risen up to annihilate, like Kali, the goddess of destruction. She smashed her wand into the attacker's back and used her nifty Death Spell.

"Get thee to Hades!" she said, and the vampire immediately ashed himself.

DEMETRIUS SNEERED at me once more. "You think you'll get away with this?"

I looked around at the ash that covered the chapel floor and shrugged. "Possibly."

He roared at me, his fury making him unstable. He knew he couldn't kill me; it would be against the Silvano Clan's orders. But he couldn't let me get away, either. I assumed either scenario would be punishable by death. Vampires aren't known for their mercy.

"Damned if you do, damned if you don't," I said, and I thought his eyes might pop right out of his head, he was so furious. Crowe swept up to where we were standing, red spellstick outstretched, with the sword-bearing Lou by her side. My own wand was sparking with magic, as if it had a mind of its own, and that mind wanted Demetrius dead.

He looked at the three of us and realized he didn't stand a chance. The two vampires flanking him took off in a blur, and he narrowed his ugly eyes at us and followed suit. I'm not sure why we let him go; perhaps to send a message.

We will not go gently.

Lou sheathed her djinn blade and holstered it on her back. Crowe slipped her spellstick into her belt, and I picked up my crossbow and clipped it to my back. Bron flew elegantly down and perched on my shoulder. We looked at each other —there was no need to smile—and we walked out of the chapel and into the soft morning light.

EPILOGUE

Outside the Moonlit Chapel, mayhem awaited us in the form of three police cars with flashing blue lights and plenty of stern-faced officers. I was worried at first, thinking that Musubarin had tracked me down to arrest me, but then I saw Morgan handcuffing Ophelia and Dylan and pushing their heads down as she forced them into one of the vehicles. Dylan was blinking in the bright light and looking confused.

"What's going on?" he was saying. "I don't understand."

I don't think he had a clue about what was happening. It was going to be an interesting trial.

I ran to my best friend. "Morgan!"

"Jax!" she said, slamming the door shut. "Thank goodness." We hugged each other, and I felt Morgan's gun pressing against my ribcage. She smelled of cheap coffee and the

Scorpion-issued leather jacket she was wearing. I didn't want to know what I smelled like. Hammerskin breath, probably. Bonfire smoke. Vampire sweat. I looked back at Izzy and Lou, but they had disappeared. Lou's words from a few days ago echoed in my head.

There's a lot you don't know, she had said. And she was right. I certainly hadn't known she was a djinn—if that is indeed what she was—and a kick-ass one, at that. Directress Copperfield had said we needed to stick together. With the future looming so dark, I was more than grateful to have her on my side.

I turned my attention to the couple in the car.

"You got them," I said.

"They were trying to escape," Morgan said. "I did a bit of running."

That's when I saw the fresh bruise on her cheekbone and pine needles in her hair. It looked like she'd done a bit more than just running.

"Well done," I said. "Case closed. You deserve a promotion. Tell the Council you're reinstating yourself as Top Dog."

"Ha," said Morgan, and rolled her eyes. Then the smile left her face. "Speaking of my position on the squad..."

"Oh *faex,*" I swore, remembering my altercation with the new—supremely annoying—wizard detective on the block,

Tilexon Musubarin. "Sorry about that. I didn't mean to kick him in the balls, I was just in a hurry to—"

Morgan's eyes widened. "You what?"

And then I laughed. I giggled, hysterically, like a schoolgirl, because I needed the relief. Morgan joined in, and for a moment it felt like we were ten years younger and without a care in the world. But then I saw the bleeding graze on her hand, and she looked at my disheveled state, and we stopped laughing.

"Are you okay?" she asked.

"Barely," I said. "How about you?"

"Same. But at least we'll be putting one killer behind bars, right?"

I nodded. "Right."

"One down, ninety-nine million to go," she joked.

"You can't look at it like that," I said, more to myself than to Morgan. "You'll drive yourself crazy."

She looked at me and smiled again. "Too late."

"THERE'S SOMETHING ELSE," Morgan said as I made my way, wearily, to my bike.

"I don't want to know," I said. "I need to sleep for a week and even then, I may not be ready to hear it."

I was craving my bed like never before. Nothing was going to stop me from going home right then and climbing into it. Nothing.

Morgan stared at me with those unnerving, unblinking eyes of hers. "I've just come from the station, right?"

"Right," I said. Honestly, I didn't want to hear it. I didn't want to know about any new dead bodies that looked like mine, about evil witches or wizards, or about Neo-Nazi orcs. I didn't want to dream of Slyden Abarim carving an old fairytale into his brother's skin, or see Liz Durison with her waxen face and leather whip. All I wanted was my mattress and my pillow and a nice warm—

Hang on, I thought. *Where the hell was Darick? He had been on his way to the chapel to help me. What had happened?*

"So," said Morgan. "I was leaving the station and there's this guy being brought in."

I frowned at her. "Yes?"

"He has this... voice."

A new sense of dread made my stomach burn.

"No." I shook my head. "No way."

The cop standing nearby climbed into the car beside us,

started the engine, and reversed out into the narrow lane, then drove away.

"So you *do* know him," Morgan said, punching me on the shoulder the way Ferra sometimes does, which made my heart ache for missing her.

"Ow!" I said, rubbing it.

"That's for not telling me about him. I knew you were hiding something! He's freaking gorgeous."

"Morgan," I said. "Get to the point, for *faex* sake!"

"So, I was on my way out, on my way here, when I hear this almighty commotion in the charge office. Your friend with the voice—"

"Darick," I said.

"Yes, Darick, that's it. Is it just me... or does that sound like a vampire name?"

I felt like pulling my hair out. "Morgan! Land the plane!"

Morgan shook her hair out of her face. "Your friend Darick was yelling at Tilexon, saying he had to let him go. Saying that you were in danger and he had to find you right away. But Moose cuffed him and slammed the door shut so hard it almost came off its hinges. Darick will be spending the night behind bars, I'm afraid."

So that's why he never arrived.

"You arrested Darick?" I asked.

"I didn't arrest him. Musubarin brought him in. He's very enthusiastic."

He was enthusiastic about arresting me too, I thought, *till I kicked him in the nads.*

"Filius Canis," I said. "He did it to get back at me."

"Maybe," said Morgan. "Or maybe Darick was breaking the law."

Poor Darick, stuck in some hellish gray cell. Who knows what dangers lurked in the Scorpion cells? I had to get him out of there. After the week I'd had, I needed Darick home, safe and sound. This was not the happy ending I was looking for.

"Can you get him out?" I asked.

Morgan looked worried. "Not today. Not without an expensive lawyer."

"But you're the captain!" I said.

"Not for long. The Council's watching my every move."

I kicked a tree, and saw that my boots were disfigured from melting over the witch hunter's bonfire.

"I'm not leaving him in there," I said. "We must be able to get him out, somehow."

"I don't think so. Moose said it's a solid case. There were witnesses. Darick was caught red-handed."

"Red-handed?" I said. "Doing what?"

Morgan shook her head, and a pine needle dropped from her bangs to the dead leaves below. She looked straight into my eyes and didn't blink. "I don't think you're going to like the answer to that."

❧

THE END

FICTION

WHEN TOMORROW CALLS

• SERIES •

(Futuristic kidnapping thriller)

The Stepford Florist: A Novelette

The Sigma Surrogate

1. Why You Were Taken

2. How We Found You

3. What Have We Done

When Tomorrow Calls Box Set: Books 1 - 3

(complete)

URBAN FANTASY

BLOOD MAGIC

(complete 6-book series)

1. The HighFire Crown

2. The Dream Drinker

3. The Witch Hunter

4. The Ember Isles

5. The Chaos Jar

6. The New Dawn Throne

CURSEBREAKER

(complete 6-book series)

1. The Dusk Reapers

2. The Haunted Portal

3. The EverShade Ring

4. The Obsidian Castle

5. The Pick Pocket's Curse

6. The Eternal Betrayal

STANDALONE NOVELS

The Memory of Water

(steamy psychological thriller)

Grey Magic

(witchy magical realism)

EverDark

(urban fantasy)

SHORT STORY COLLECTIONS

Sticky Fingers

Sticky Fingers 2

Sticky Fingers 3

Sticky Fingers 4

Sticky Fingers 5

Sticky Fingers 6

Sticky Fingers: The Complete Collection:

Books 1 - 6: 72 Short Stories

NON-FICTION

The Underachieving Ovary

(memoir)

The Indie Author Game Plan